UFO's, Aliens and Religion

UFO's, Aliens and Religion

by *Michael Roses*

ISBN 9780645719000

Dedicated to all good people on planet Earth

Chapter 1

The alarm sounded. It was six thirty in the morning and today was his 40th birthday. Married to a beautiful woman and a beautiful person and with two daughters aged six and five, his life should be one of bliss. Indeed, it could have been - and it still could be that way too.

That might be his call!

The alarm had not woken him from his late night, so she did.

"Wakey wakies! Birthday boy! Rise and shine."

He rolled over with a groan and sheepishly opened his eyes to gaze upon her beautiful face. A face he did not deserve!

"Guess what mummy has for you, a little card – and this" as she handed him a small parcel.

He sat up in his bed and gave her a kiss, then proceeded to open his card. Another humorous card, of course, for she always liked to humor him.

He read the front cover, a picture of the Phantom talking with a bedraggled native.

"If it's any consolation, you don't look 40", said the Phantom to the native.

He knew there was something very funny inside because she already had a smile on her dial, so he opened it with great expectation.

It was the Phantom again and he said:

"But you used to!"

He had to laugh and she giggled too, so he gave her another kiss and then looked back at the clock.

1

"Better get into it I suppose – another long day ahead after what happened at the meeting last night", explaining why he had arrived home after 11pm.

He showered and dressed while she made him his favorite breakfast – bacon and eggs with a beef sausage, a fried tomato and a generous serve of mushrooms, served on toast. Topped off with a slice of toast and raspberry jam and two cups of coffee! It was a great way to start his day and at this early stage, no sign of the end of planet Earth. For today was Friday the 9th day of February in the year 2035.

Life can be very difficult within the walls of a top law firm. A lot of stress, a lot of uncertainty, a lot of client pressure and an ongoing wrestling match against opposing lawyers over the letter of the law.

He caught the usual train at 07:40 and walked the walk to his Second Avenue office of Hansen and Richards and entered the foyer to the lift well, for a meeting to start at 8am – earlier than usual.

He didn't realize it but she was right behind him. They got into the lift together with a few others, the door closed and then he realized that she was there.

They remained silent, occasionally glancing at each other with a smirk.

As luck would have it, the others left the lift first and left them alone to each other.

"Happy birthday to you, happy birthday to you, happy birthday dear Michael, happy birthday to you! Everything okay when you got home last night?" as she sidled up to him.

"Yeah, it was cool – nothing suspected. I told Julie about the case and how huge it will be. That did the trick. What about at your end ... ah ... Graham?"

"Sound asleep he was and still when I left this morning. No problem."

"Chrissy - you realize that we just cannot let this get out of the bag, you know ... ah ... we are both married."

"Don't worry, birthday boy, I'll just settle for the extra passion in my life."

The lift stopped and they walked rather platonically toward the conference room and took their seats – opposite one another of course – just for the occasional glance across the table.

The chief executive officer, Gerry Macklin, made the big announcement!

"Today will probably be the biggest day in the history of Hansen and Richards. For today we lodge writs with the Supreme Court to initiate the class action against this country's largest and wealthiest property developers for alleged price fixing in the retail industry. So today the world just might start to end for some of them."

"Oh ... I almost forgot, congratulations to Michael McIntyre who turns forty today. Happy birthday to Michael."

Everybody clapped and wished Michael a happy birthday. He smiled and nodded his acknowledgement.

"As you will all be aware this action has come about because a number of former retailers have banded together to make this claim, that many years ago the developers of shopping centers put their heads together, through what has been spuriously called the "property council", to inflate retail

3

rents to arbitrarily exorbitant levels. The upshot of this is that rents in the retail sector virtually doubled, even trebled, across the board in the few years between 1988 and 1990 and have remained so ever since."

"We now have better than anecdotal evidence from certain persons who became property developers, by virtue of their accumulating wealth by legitimate means, who gained membership entry to the property council but were aghast at the blatant price fixing dialogue of some of the major players in the retail industry."

"Some of these developers refused to compromise their values or their integrity by acquiescing with the major players and have now turned against them. They are willing to cooperate with the plaintiff group, which is now comprised of several hundred signatories to this class action."

"Ah Gerry … won't these renegade developers be seen by the courts to have an ulterior motive in trying to bring down some of the major players – that to extirpate them would make more room for themselves in the industry?"

"That, Bob, could well be the view of the major players who are about to be sued but that is not a matter for the courts, no, the courts will be focusing on whether the evidence that comes to light is sufficiently substantive to support the statement of claim – that blatant price fixing has occurred."

"So just how big will this case be Gerry? Retailing is huge, everywhere now, there are enormous shopping centers right through every state."

"That's correct Rebecca, this case has the potential to be the biggest legal stoush in history, there is enormous wealth in retailing and the defendants may seem to have the upper hand in dollar terms but we will be arguing for a waiver of limitations based on the grounds of unconscionable conduct which will effectively open the door for every former retailer who was duped over a period of more than twenty years. So effectively there could actually be more than one million respondents to the action, as plaintiffs. This means our fighting fund will be huge too because a lot of people who were dispossessed have now made good and are willing to sink a lot of money into this cause. Initial estimates put to us by the Independent Retailers Association are in the vicinity of fifty billion dollars, depending on just how much the courts are prepared to compensate."

"Gerry if limitations are not waived and we are restricted to representing those parties who are still within the limitations period, do you have any estimate of just how many respondents there would be then?"

"At this point of time Dave, we would estimate at least twenty thousand will come on board once we advertise the case via the normal media channels, because there are or were literally hundreds in every major shopping center ever built in America, but a successful application to waive limitations would probably bring in many times that number. A lot of people were only in the industry for a short time because their businesses were virtually insolvent from the time they first commenced trading, simply because of the artificial rents and other overheads."

"Strangely, it seems that we here in the United States inherited this problem from Australia where it all took a very nasty twist for the worse when the property developers virtually seconded middlemen to do their dirty work for them and here I am referring to franchisors! I say that because through franchising and the franchisors the developers have access to all of the trading figures for every tenant and they know exactly how much gross profit each tenant makes and therefore, exactly how much can be exacted from those tenants to leave them with a predetermined level of net profit."

"Prior to all this taking place retailers themselves could make a reasonable profit from operating their businesses, in the traditional way, knowing that they had exclusive knowledge of their revenue and expenses and their profitability. The developers and landlords didn't really care if the retailers made a substantial profit as long as they were able to pay their rent."

"So, what changed?"

"Well, Chrissy, it seems that in Australia the developers got smart and decided that they would reap the benefit of having two or three traders operating in the same product lines and thereby erode the profits that retailers were able to make but in the process pick up the rents from the additional premises."

"So rather than have one retailer in say, haberdashery, making a profit of two hundred thousand dollars a year, they could have two retailers making half as much profit but collect double the rental income. Or even three retailers making less than seventy thousand dollars each per annum."

"Yes Chrissy you've hit the nail on the head right there but they didn't stop there, they have virtually taken that to the "nth" degree by introducing multiple tenancies in every single retail line and will continue to do so until they reduce every tenant to a predetermined profit level. Above that, they add enormous value to their property profile by virtually converting money that used to be profit for retailers into rents for landlords."

"And now they know exactly how far they can push that because through the franchisors they have all of the trading figures."

As he spoke Michael's mind drifted away into the clouds – he kept glancing at Chrissy sitting opposite him and going over and over, in his mind, those intimate moments of the night before, when she was with him in the office and she allowed him to gaze upon her body. He had been totally enthralled by her body, as she was just the second woman that he had ever made love with and his wife, being of a very conservative Christian upbringing, was quite prudish in such things.

He kept going over it in his mind! 'So this is what women really look like. Golly! Can't wait to be with her again - maybe tonight with a bit of luck'.

"Michael!"

"Michael!" Came a more stern demand from Gerry. "Would you mind answering Dave's question, please".

Michael was taken aback by Gerry bringing him out of his daydream and without being sure of what had been asked of him, he improvised a rather nebulous response that seemed plausible enough, whatever it was they had asked him.

"Ah ... look, I wouldn't want to pre-empt any conclusions that people here might decide upon so I really would prefer to do a thorough check of legal precedent before making any statements about the implications of price fixing, you know, there are so many cases that have been proven in the positive but even more that have been rejected, so ... ah ... I would like you to leave that with me until tomorrow and I will brief you all on that then."

Gerry came back to the line of discussion before he had asked Michael for his view.

"This complicity with the franchisors and the access it provides to all financial details of the retailers is the very reason why, you will notice, that virtually all retailers in major shopping centers now belong to a franchise group."

"But aren't there considerable benefits from belonging to a franchise, don't they provide the expertise and knowledge to the franchisee?"

"That's the fallacy of it all, Michael – the franchisors themselves make enormous profits because of their set establishment and annual fees and their watertight legal contracts protect them in every way if the retailer - the franchisee - doesn't make it. Even worse, with so much money to be made in franchising, by the franchisors, only the prospective franchisors who are willing to play ball with the property developers in every conceivable way will be accepted into the system. The franchisors make a handsome profit, the developers make a fortune, but every year we see thousands of retailers driven into bankruptcy. We actually now have several former franchisors who were extirpated from the retail system by the developers for not complying, come forward to assist our cause".

"Apart from that I have been assured by the people within the mathematics department at Harvard University that they can utilize the mathematics of correlation and inference to demonstrate how the increases in rents and overheads across the board defy all natural or pre-existing progressions and could, therefore, only have come about by complicity. We also have a few people who were in attendance at various national conferences of the members of the property council who still have documents that were presented to the conference at the time – and here I am talking way back in the late eighties – that literally set down the estimates of how the increases ought to be implemented, so it is likely to be a long and dirty fight but we have a lot in our favor at the moment."

"This all sounds so sinister, why hasn't something been done about all of this at the political level?"

"Rebecca, the property developers have the politicians in their pockets – they all make sizeable annual donations to the politicians' electoral campaign funding."

"That's right Dave, this problem is so far out of hand now that only court action is going to bring about the political will to institute the necessary controls to end the complicity between the major players. Which is why we have decided to take on this case, as you know, Hansen and Richards has not exactly had money, nor profit making, at the top of its mission statement."

"Michael and Chrissy, you will be at the forefront of the information accumulation and ... ah ... needless to say, you will need to spend some long hours together on this."

Michael and Chrissy looked at each other and nodded their heads in approval with a tad of subtle smiling.

"Now, I want to thank you all for coming in earlier than usual today and as this will be an intense session, let's all take a short coffee break because when we return we will hear from a visitor, the President of the Independent Retailers and his lawyers, who will provide us with some more detail about just what the retailers have been experiencing for the last twenty years."

As the group arose from the table Michael and Chrissy glanced at each other and he gave a subtle lateral nod of his head as if to indicate they should go separate ways for the coffee break.

"Hey Michael, are you good for a cappuccino downstairs at Dizzy's?"

"Sure Bob that would be great. I sure need something to kick me along after last night's effort."

"You didn't work back last night, did you?"

"Oh ... just for a short while but I had a lot of stuff to do at home."

Michael and Bob made their way towards the lift and Rebecca and Chrissy headed towards the staff room for the usual Tuesday morning update on nappy rash, soap operas and recipes.

After ordering two cappuccinos Michael decided to seek a little assurance from his workmate Bob to placate a little guilt about his rendezvous with Chrissy the night before. Bob was a few years older and he, himself, had a lovely wife named Rachael. They had been together since they married in their early twenties.

"So it's the big "four zero" today Michael, well congratulations brother, you've made it this far, now you can start the downhill slide, eh."

Yeah I suppose so. Ah ... Bob, just on that, I hope you don't mind me asking but, do you and Rachael still feel very much ... ah ... passion in your life, in middle age?"

"Huh, middle age, eh, well this may come as a surprise to you but I still feel very much like a young person, but to answer your question, some women become more sexual once they get past forty you know. So, what did you really get up to last night?"

"What makes you think I got up to something?"

"You avoided eye contact when I asked you the first time. Don't tell me you've got something going on outside of home!"

"The wily old fox strikes again, eh."

Michael turned and looked around the room at the other customers to gather his thoughts, for he was in quite a quandary about what to divulge to his friend Bob.

"Things at home aren't exactly what they should be, you know ... ah ... Julie is a great wife and mother but, in recent months she hasn't had the same passion that most men might need in their life. Which is the reason why I asked you Bob ... about yourself and Rachael."

"So you do have a liaison going on with somebody else, Michael. I've got to tell you, I am more than just a little surprised, you know, you and Julie are regarded by everybody at the firm as epitomizing a model couple Michael."

"Yeah, I suppose we would be but, Julie comes from a very conservative religious upbringing, you know, Baptist parents heavily involved in Sunday school. I had to placate them fairly early in the piece after meeting Julie that my own Catholic upbringing put us on the same playing field, even though they regard the Catholic Church as having a lot to answer for,

11

especially in recent years with what has come out of the priesthood. Julie has always been quite prudish and would be happy with making love just once a week, even less than that and ... ah ... I suppose I could use some love and affection at least two or three times a week. You know how it is with all the stress from the office. I had no intentions of ever being disloyal but, sometimes you cross paths with the right ... with another person ... and it just happens."

"Well there are plenty of women out there in the same boat and a lot of single women too are willing to go along with a married man. I mean, take one very well-known professional golfer, for example. According to one report he seems to have had a fling with over a hundred women while he was married to his wife, but, most of them were single women and probably all of them knew that he was a married man. I find that really surprising that so many single women could have an affair with a man who is married. I have to wonder whether there are any single women out there that he put the hard word on and they said no, because they knew he was married."

"Yeah, fair point Bob, but I suppose we will never know, eh."

"Probably not! So how do you reconcile this recent liaison of yours with your own spiritual beliefs, Michael – having been raised as a Catholic yourself."

"Well ... I've got to admit that I haven't been your model Catholic for a long time now. I stopped going to church while I was at college, before I met Julie and ah ... I suppose when you get to know what is really going on in the world you start to question a lot of what you were brought up with. I mean, take the arms race for example and the military budget and all of the power plays that are going on between the corporate rich, the military and Congress, it's ... ah ... all for money you know. Any person can become quite disillusioned with the realities of life and quite justifiably call a lot of beliefs systems into question."

"So you read *The Power Elite* by C. Wright Mills."

"Yeah that was part of our political sociology stream, sure. If you want to be a good lawyer you've got to know what the bastards are really up to, eh? I suppose for me it has been a problem of seeing the relevance of the church in this day and age. I mean, when you go to church and they read from the scripture about loaves and fishes or water becoming wine you know how the story ends as soon as they start to read it – because you've heard it dozens of times before. It doesn't ... ah ... have a lot of relevance or meaning for me today. And Julie's church, with all those happy clappers carrying on the way they do, singing out loud and making strange noises, it all just seems so artificial to me."

"Pentecostals eh? Well I'm not surprised to hear you say that. I think that most people who are conventional, down to earth Christians would find the antics of Pentecostal churches rather weird. You can't doubt their fervor, but it just seems to be misplaced, somehow."

"So, as an Anglican, have you always practiced your faith Bob?"

"I've got to tell you that I went through the same phase that you have when I was younger but, came back to a better understanding of the relevance of God in my life when somebody gave me a copy of Good News for Modern Man –

which I actually read even though I thought I knew it all already."

"Why would that have an impact on you?"

"I realized the importance of the things that Jesus said."

"Like what?"

"Well you tell me – you think you've heard it all before and that is why you think the church lacks relevance to you. So why don't you tell me what you recall about what Jesus said."

"Well – he said to love your neighbor as yourself."

"Yes he certainly did!" Bob then paused for a moment to give Michael some time to think of something else. "And?"

Well he told parables, didn't he? Ah ... the parable of the ten lepers!"

"That wasn't a parable Michael - that was actually a miracle that the Lord performed."

"Well there was the parable of the Good Shepherd and the parable of the Prodigal Son?"

"Very interesting that you should mention those two Michael – probably the two most important parables that Jesus ever told."

"Really! Why do you say that?"

"Well, think about it Michael – one of the sheep strays away from the flock. What does the good shepherd do about that? Does he wait to see if that lost sheep returns?"

"No, he goes out looking for that lost sheep."

"That's right, he does!"

"And he leaves all the others behind to the mercy of the wolves."

"But he knew that those who stayed in the flock were safe, Michael. So what is the meaning of that? It means that in some peculiar way God regards every one of us as being just as important as everybody else put together."

"If that's possible!"

"Well if you believe that God has such enormous power that he created the universe and everything within it, you should accept that anything would be possible for him. But the parable of the Good Shepherd also means that we Christians have a responsibility to be pro-active in going out there to seek out those who need help from us – like these forlorn people who have been dispossessed by the property developers."

"Is that why we are launching ourselves into this hornets' nest against the property developers?"

"Well you should realize that Gerry and the other senior partners have always regarded their Christian mission in life as being the driving force behind their pro-bono work, which is probably why they came to us first, although this case should actually be quite lucrative for us. Those plaintiffs constitute a large and wealthy force now. It was also one of the reasons that you were chosen for the position you hold within the firm, Michael – that you were seen as being a person with that Christian ethic."

"And the Prodigal Son?"

"God is always there, willing to accept anybody who turns towards him – or turns back to him. Just remember that when that father saw his son coming, from a distance, he didn't wait for the boy to walk the remaining distance home. He ran to the boy - then he hugged the boy and kissed him. Then he threw the banquet to celebrate."

"And remember one thing that the Lord said, Michael – no man can have two masters – he will love one and despise the other. You cannot serve God and money. I can tell you that nothing manifests that as well as our sacred institution of law."

Michael nodded his head. "I could certainly concur with that view. We had better be heading back now."

"So! Is she anybody I know?"

"I think I had better keep that to myself actually."

Bob just gave a wry smile as if to allude to his assumption that Michael's lover was, in fact, somebody that he knew. He was already suspecting that she was somebody from the office – after all, there were dozens of women in the firm in law and administration and hundreds more in the same building. Michael and Bob made their way back into the office and took up their seats in the conference room. Everybody was there except Rebecca.

Chapter 2

Gerry gave them a few minutes to chat then decided to proceed.

"Has anybody seen Rebecca these last few minutes?"

"She was going to walk down towards 41st street to the news stand – I think she needed to buy some aspirin because she's not feeling one hundred per cent."

"Thanks Chrissy. Well it seems our guests are not here yet either so if anybody has any issues to raise before they arrive, now is the time."

The door opened and Rebecca made her entry. She closed the door and just stood there and leaned backward against the door, looking up at the ceiling.

"Rebecca our guests are not here yet – could you take your seat please. Dave has raised the question of whether we are going to do this on a no win-no fee basis."

"They're here!" Rebecca said.

"Wonderful, would you allow them to come in, please?"

Rebecca simply stood there leaning backwards against the door staring straight ahead across the room and toward the windows.

"They're here!" she said again, blinking as she looked sideways from one side of the room to the other, breathing deeply in a seemingly disoriented state.

"Well, will you please allow them to come in?"

Rebecca seemed to snap out of her dazed state, looked at the people in the room, looked at the television screen adorning the wall then looked at the television controller on the table. She took two steps forward, picked up the controller, pointed it at the screen with her left hand and clicked the power button.

As the television screen powered up everybody turned toward the screen. The telecast picked up on a scene in the street involving a CXN News reporter.

"... there are people now pouring out of the buildings in this vicinity and running in every direction and I can tell you this is pandemonium here right now."

"They" Rebecca said quite indignantly, "are here."

"What is this?" said Bob.

The CXN reporter had stopped a young man who appeared to be in his twenties.

"... yeah I was just over there, walking along the sidewalk there and I heard an airplane that was coming in to land so I looked up and saw that it was an Airbus 380 so I watched it for a while and then ... I saw this other thing in the sky above the 380 and it was, kind of, a small, round disc about the size of a pea. Then just a few seconds later it was getting larger man, and it was about the size of a golf ball and then it was about the size of a pumpkin so I realized it was like descending until it came right down to where it is now and ... it's just been sitting there above that building for about ten minutes now and ... ah ... well it's huge man."

"Yeah it just came straight down to there, above that building and stopped, man, right where it is now. I saw it too" interjected another bystander.

The reporter turned back toward the camera.

"We have just heard from one young man who is an eyewitness to this extraordinary event here in New York. Now, ... for those of you who have just tuned in we are here in front of the United Nations Headquarters on 1st Avenue where an aircraft of some type has descended to a position directly above the United Nations Headquarters. There is already quite a lot of panic here in the streets of New York City."

"Is this a terrorist attack or something?" asked Michael as they all watched the wide screen.

"Oh no, not again!"

"As you can see now on your screen this circular aircraft is just hovering directly above the United Nations building and has been hovering there in that position for about ten minutes or more now. At this point of time, we have absolutely no idea what this aircraft is nor where it has come from but ... ah ... there is a huge crowd gathering here right now as we speak in front of the building and all the way along the plaza towards 45th street and 46th street and there is a lot of confusion and quite some mayhem here right now. I can see from here that a lot of people are now streaming out of office buildings and running away from this vicinity. I guess a lot of people headed for the subway or their cars to vacate this precinct. But right here everybody is talking to somebody and it seems everyone is trying to get a handle on what is going on here, because we have never seen anything like this before".

"George, did you say this is a circular aircraft? Are you saying that this appears to be some kind of unidentified flying object?"

"This is definitely a UFO, Barbara, because this aircraft is a circular disc shape and it is quite sizeable ... ah ... maybe about fifty feet or so in diameter and there are, there are lights beneath the aircraft that are rotating - we see red, blue and yellow lights spinning around at the base of this aircraft".

"And George this aircraft is stationary as if it is hovering above the UN building?"

"That's correct Barbara, I have never seen anything like this before. The aircraft is just sitting there as if it is some type of hovercraft or drone, or as if it is defying gravity, though obviously a hovercraft could not actually do something like this at that height, at that altitude, because this aircraft is ... ah ... probably about six hundred feet above the ground."

"Now just as we speak, we hear some jets approaching and, oh my God, there are two fighter jets flying over now and the noise is becoming deafening."

He pauses while two jets fly overhead.

"What the hell is this?" remarked Gerry.

"That looked like two air force F22A Raptors, that have done a flyover and now we see them separating and starting to turn, maybe they are going to come back again. They were flying quite low, probably only at one thousand feet and really moving I can tell you but the spacecraft did ..."

"George can we get this straight, is there any way that this aircraft, or what appears to be an aircraft, may be a drone or some type of hoax or an object that has been placed into position from somewhere on the ground?"

"Well, let me tell you Tom and I was just about to say, that when those two Raptors flew over that aircraft that is hovering there suddenly ascended to about two thousand feet in just a fraction of a second and then came back down again to where it was and there is no way that anything we know of could do that type of thing."

20

"Those Raptors are heading back this way but now they are flying much slower than they were the first time, they have definitely slowed down to a crawl and they are about to fly overhead again but one on each side of the UN building, one on each side of this aircraft that is still hovering ... no, wait ... this aircraft, dare I call this a spaceship ... has once again ascended quite abruptly to about two thousand feet as the Raptors fly beneath it and ... now it has suddenly come back down again to where it was and, I can tell you, that nothing, nothing that we know of could do that type of maneuver, so this is definitely not some kind of a hoax nor connected to the ground because this spaceship ... ah ... aircraft has just performed a couple of maneuvers that are really quite extraordinary. I've never seen anything like it."

Back at the office everybody watched in astonishment.

"Is this for real?" asked Dave.

"This is CXN so what do you think, of course it's for real, this is happening right now right here in New York" said Rebecca.

"How can this be possible?" said Chrissy.

"Guys can we listen in to what is going on here please" said Gerry.

It was now just before 9am.

The news was now permeating its way through the White House in Washington DC and would very quickly make its way to the top. The U.S. President Mr. Brett Bahama - who was inaugurated less than two weeks earlier following the abdication of President Antony Blinken for health reasons - was in a meeting with the Joint Chiefs of Staff. They were determining their initial response to an incident in the South

China Sea, where a U.S. destroyer was fired upon by a Chinese fighter just twelve miles from China's ever-expanding artificial islands. The U.S. response would need to be forceful – perhaps with the assignment of an aircraft carrier to the area - but they needed to assess how the Chinese would respond to an increase in U.S. military presence in the area.

The door opened. It was the conference room secretary.

"Excuse me sir ... ah ... I know you gave strict orders for there to be no interruption."

"That's right I did" said the President just a little indignantly.

"Whatever it is you feel you need to say, Erica, I am asking you if it can possibly wait. We have an immediate crisis on our hands here."

"Ah ... no sir I think not! The United States, sir, may be under attack!"

The President and all members of the Joint Chiefs of Staff immediately arose from their seats and moved briskly toward the door from where they would make their way to a secure facility below the White House. As they walked out the conference room door and headed along the corridor the President asked the secretary the pertinent question.

"Erica, tell me what we are dealing with here."

"It is in New York sir – some type of aircraft we have never seen before."

"Pray tell what type of aircraft have we never seen before?"

"It's a UFO sir."

The President stopped. Everybody stopped behind him – in concertina fashion.

"What?"

"Yes sir it is a genuine unidentifiable flying aircraft, sir and we have reason to believe that this is a genuine extra-terrestrial aircraft sir. It is presently hovering above the United Nations building sir."

"You have got to be kidding me!"

The President turned to look at his Joint Chiefs and saw a lot of blank, dazed faces.

"Did you all hear that?"

"Yes sir" was the unanimous response. They had all heard the secretary.

"I'll believe it when I see it" replied the Chief of the Air Force.

They moved on toward the lift that would take them below ground. All ten of them were able to occupy the lift at once.

"How much do you know already?"

"Sir, I have seen it with my own eyes on CXN and the aircraft was twice approached by Raptor jets and both times, sir, the aircraft performed a maneuver that was seemingly impossible sir."

"What type of maneuver?"

"Ah ... it went from about six hundred feet to approximately two thousand feet in less than one second sir."

"Holy shit!"

The Airforce Chief had expressed his surprise.

"But then it came back down to where it was previously."

"So has it done anything in terms of any hostility?"

"No, nothing sir, it is simply hovering there above the U.N. building sir."

The lift door opened and a coterie of aides were waiting to escort the team to the secure communication facility, where television screens were showing the live coverage. The President and his team gathered around a very large screen and looked on with amazement. There, right before them on the large screen was a live view of the spacecraft hovering in the sky above the U.N. building.

"My God! Would you look at that!"

The CXN's George Bowman was talking.

"... I guess if this UFO was hostile, they could have caused a lot of damage and destruction here already because our very best aircraft, the F22A Raptors, were treated with disdain here when they approached. Those two pilots must have got quite a surprise when they saw the UFO perform that maneuver. Of course, they would never have seen anything like that before."

The President's entourage stared at the vision of the screen in disbelief for this was a defining moment in the history for all, for the presiding feeling was that, even though they were not so surprised at the fact that a UFO was here – but that the cat had been let out of the bag. The mood was sullen – no longer would they be able to talk of weather balloons nor Venus nor hallucinations to account for so many UFO sightings.

"Excuse me sir, we ... ah ... have reason to believe that these alien visitors will not be hostile sir."

"And why would you say that?"

"It's because they have been here for quite some time now, sir, ... ah ... ever since Roswell, sir."

"Are you kidding me Charles? When were you planning on telling me of this?"

"Not so soon after your inauguration, sir, as you have situations to deal with in Syria and Afghanistan sir."

"And I suppose you are going to tell me that former Presidents have known of this."

"Ah .. yes sir, ever since President Eisenhower sir. He sent the CIA in to Area 51 and to S4 to investigate and to report to him and they reported that the U.S. Government had no jurisdiction there, sir."

"No jurisdiction? What on earth did they mean by that?"

"They found that the aliens were in charge of S4 sir."

"And they kept that a secret from the people?"

"Yes sir but President Obama alluded to the same when he was interviewed by Jimmy Kimmel sir. Mr. Obama said 'the aliens exercise strict control over us' and 'I can't reveal anything' and when Mr. Kimmel pointed out that President Clinton had publicly denied any alien presence, Mr. Obama responded by stating 'well that's what we're instructed to say', sir."

"That's because the people of Earth have never been ready for this Mr. President."

"So when was somebody going to inform me?"

"Usually after a couple of months in the Presidency sir."

"I see! Erica would you please summon Air Force One for me to travel to New York City and I need to leave now."

"Excuse me sir I would recommend against that – I feel strongly that you need to stay here until we ascertain what we are dealing with here."

"Sir I agree with the Chairman, we cannot afford to lose our commander-in-chief of the armed forces."

"Thank you for your concern gentlemen but, no, this situation will be causing havoc everywhere now, not just here in the States but all around the world. I really need to show some leadership here, that is absolutely imperative. You all know the score on the backup plan should I find myself in any form of peril. The Vice-President must not accompany me. You should also give consideration to an evacuation to Cheyenne Mountain."

"Sir, if you must go immediately, may I recommend that we accompany the Air Force One with two Raptors?"

"Yes thank you – that would be a good idea. Ah … can you make that four Raptors please."

"Yes sir!"

The President hastily left the conference room taking nothing with him as he made his way to the transport helicopter that would take him to Air Force One. He could be in New York City by 10:30am.

Meanwhile the CXN coverage continued.

"George was there any indication that the air force jets were preparing to fire upon this aircraft?"

"No, Barbara, there was no sign of any aggression at this time but as we speak the Raptors are heading away into the distance but, I don't know if you can hear that other noise ... guys can we get a take on this ... there are, what looks like, six Apache helicopters just coming into sight now from the horizon and they are probably just a minute or so from being right here where this spaceship is, still hovering over the United Nations building."

"Now we see a lot of people here, exiting the buildings in this vicinity and ... ah ... a lot of people starting to run away from this area in all directions now."

He manages to stop a man who is rushing by.

"Excuse me sir, where are you going to right now?"

"I am going to get into my car and drive away from here to Brooklyn to get my wife and children and we are going to get out of New York as soon as possible. I was here for September eleven and we are not going through that again."

The man rushed off, so the reporter stopped another man rushing by.

"Excuse me sir, where are you going to?"

"I'm just gonna get the hell out of here man this is looking pretty much like Independence Day to me."

The reporter turns back to the camera.

"Well Barbara, Tom, there you have it, there are more and more people now running out of buildings and into the streets and a lot of people here are in a big hurry. This is starting to look like a scene from a disaster movie already, though we also see that the crowd that is gathering here to watch this event unfolding is growing bigger by the minute. There must be over a thousand people here now just standing here and watching this and those Apache helicopters are taking up positions around this spacecraft or aircraft. The Apache's have formed a circular formation each of them about one hundred yards away from this spacecraft and they have the spacecraft completely surrounded now. People here are holding hands and embracing each other, this whole situation really is quite dramatic now."

Back in the office the lawyers were starting to worry.

"Gerry, do you mind if we call an end to this meeting now? I would like to go home to be with Julie and the kids and to make sure they are not too worried about this."

Chrissy looked across at Michael as if a knife had just pierced her heart with jealousy. Within an instant she felt that she would rather be going to a loving home with Michael, rather than going home to her husband Graham. She didn't realize she would feel this way until now.

"That's probably the best thing to do right now Michael and let's just see how this incident pans out for the rest of the day. Perhaps we all just return to work on Monday morning if this gets sorted out, somehow."

"I think I'll just stay here for a while and watch how this unfolds if that's okay with you Gerry" said Chrissy, rather hoping to entice Michael into staying back with her.

"Sure Chrissy, you know how to let yourself out of the office if we close for the day but make sure you don't leave yourself in harm's way, okay!"

"Well I'm staying here too for now because ... this is really weird what is happening here – I need to watch this for a while."

"That's okay Dave, you stay as long as you like – as for me I'm going home to Narelle."

Dave picked up the remote controller, turned the volume up again and returned to the screen, again picking up the coverage.

Chrissy looked at Michael.

"Actually, I think I might make the walk downtown to watch this first-hand for myself. If this is going to be the end, I would like it to be quick. Anyone care to join me?"

"Yes, Chrissy, if you don't mind I'll walk part of the way with you."

Michael and Chrissy left the room together and made their way towards the United Nations building. Meanwhile CXN had just put its own chopper into the air and it was approaching the scene, with reporter Rod Saunders on board.

"... only about a minute away now from where it will take up a vantage point not far from the Air Force Apache helicopters and we have our man Rod Saunders on board our CXN helicopter. Rod, tell us – how does the scene look as you make your way towards the limits of the no-fly zone there?"

"Well firstly, Tom, you have alluded there to the fact that we have been informed by the Air Force that a no-fly zone is now in place in the immediate vicinity above the United Nations building and we have been directly informed that we cannot venture within five hundred yards of the air space above the building and that area is, in fact, occupied by the Apache helicopters. Of course, our cameras can zoom in to the action here and ... ah ... right now we see that the Apache helicopters have this very strange aircraft completely surrounded."

"Thank you, Rod Saunders, can you please keep us informed of anything that changes there at the scene of this extraordinary event. Now we believe that U.S. President Brett Bahama left Washington in an Air Force jet as soon as news of this event broke here on CXN and is presently heading toward New York City and he is expected to touch down here in New York in just over an hour from now. The President has called for a public address in the media conference room at 10:45 this morning and, we are pleased to advise that, we here at CXN will have pride of place in the media room. Just repeating, that U.S. President, Brett Bahama, is on his way already, to New York City."

"And now we welcome our night presenter Alex Dwyer back into the CXN studio having left just a few hours earlier after a long stint here but, obviously, Alex, you have decided to come back to the studio to assist us in the coverage of this event."

"Barbara, when I arrived home just half an hour ago my wife was already in hysterics watching the events unfolding here at CXN and I just turned around and headed straight back to the studio because, I have got to tell you, I have been in television for more than thirty years now as you know and I have never seen anything like this. This is like something out of a Hollywood movie, it's unbelievable."

"Well we certainly appreciate you returning to assist us in this coverage after working all night. Let's check again with Rod Saunders."

"Thank you, Tom Lowry, but I wouldn't miss this for anything. I might hasten to add that in circumstances like these I would question the wisdom of the President in coming here to New York before we can be sure that there are not going to be any hostilities here. I think a lot of people would be thinking of scenes like those we saw in the Independence Day movie, right now."

"We heard exactly that earlier from a gentleman in the street but let's just check back with our man in the sky Rod Saunders right now. Rod this unidentified aircraft made some strange maneuvers earlier that seemed quite incredible from what our man George Bowman had to tell, can you just let us know for now, is there any sign of activity at all coming from this aircraft or is it still just hovering there?"

"As we speak, Barbara, the aircraft or UFO – call it what you like – is simply in a hovering position about one hundred feet above the roof of the United Nations building – that puts it about six hundred feet above the ground – and there is no sign at the moment of any activity except that it is surrounded by the Air Force choppers. This scene is rather reminiscent of an old western style standoff here at the moment."

"Rod can you imagine how those chopper pilots would be feeling right now not knowing what they might be dealing with here?"

"Understandably Tom, I would imagine the people in the Apache's would be feeling quite some trepidation and very apprehensive and bewildered right now because they would never have dealt with anything like this before and, when you are in a helicopter, if something goes wrong there is only one way to go and that is down. I suspect the choppers that have this aircraft surrounded would now be in constant communications with defense authorities and I dare say with the Secretary of Defense and probably also the White House, because we have never seen anything like this before I can tell you. As you know Tom, since September eleven two thousand and one, any occurrence like this raises the attention of everybody at the highest level all the way to the President, within just a few minutes."

"Rod, can you tell us, please, what else you can see from the CXN helicopter, perhaps any activity on the ground as a result of this event."

"Barbara, from where we are we do see quite a lot of movement on the ground – there are a lot of people in the streets of New York City now and a lot of people running and there looks to be quite a substantial amount of traffic now heading over the Brooklyn Bridge already and ... ah ... this could become very chaotic very quickly if authorities don't react to this on the ground as well. This is going to need some control."

"Thank you Rod for that and now we have some pictures coming in from our overseas correspondents from places like Paris and London and Sydney and already the word of this extraordinary event is spreading right throughout the world. Local television stations all around the world are starting to pick up on our CXN coverage of this event and you can see there that large crowds of people are starting to gather in the city centers in London and Paris to view this on large screens.

So we cross live now to our reporter in London Sue Driscoll, good morning Sue can you tell us how people there are reacting to what is happening here in New York."

"Yes Barbara, as you know it is actually early afternoon here in London and already thousands of people have gathered here to view these scenes on the large screens in Trafalgar Square and people are seeking solace from each other and holding hands but most are just staring upwards transfixed to the screen, many seemingly worried, even distressed at the prospect that we may have, indeed, been visited by – who knows – quite possibly an alien race."

"Sue we have seen a lot of people here in New York take to the streets already heading out of the city, presumably going to their homes to move away, can you tell us are there any signs of pandemonium there in London at the moment?"

"No, Alex, everybody here is transfixed on the screen and probably because here in London they wouldn't feel the same level of threat that, understandably, New Yorkers would be feeling right now. The people here are standing around in small groups and constantly chatting to each other. I suppose everybody wants to know what others are thinking about this extraordinary event and, perhaps seeking assurance that others don't see this as some kind of enormous calamity. The crowd here is growing by the minute and there must be about ten thousand people here now in Trafalgar Square in London. I might just ask these two young women and two young men over here what they think about this. Excuse me miss, Sue Driscoll for CXN in the United States, would you mind telling me what you are thinking about this right now please."

"Wow this is really cool, I knew this would happen one day – I mean everybody knows there have been UFO's flying around for years now."

"Yeah I think it's fantastic that something like this has finally happened because, you know, there's been all the cover up going on ever since Roswell, everybody knows that."

"And you sir."

"As long as they aren't hostile I think it's great, let's see who they are and where they come from. Wherever that is, I wouldn't mind going there but it's starting to look like Jesus Christ was a fraud already."

"And you miss?"

"I'm not so sure, you know, I'm a Christian and I don't want to think that there are aliens out there all over the universe. I always thought we were rather unique in God's eyes."

Michael and Chrissy had made their way quickly towards the scene and just as they arrived at the scene and as they gazed upwards at the spacecraft - still hovering quite still and motionless - Chrissy felt that she needed some comforting from Michael. She placed her left arm around his waist and rested her head on his shoulder. He looked at her and kissed her on her forehead. She looked up at him and it was obvious that she was slightly terrified by this event. He tried to placate her by placing his arm around her, he then kissed her on the lips – a brief but passionate kiss.

"Well Barbara, Alex, Tom there you have heard it from three young people here in Trafalgar Square in London - some rather excited about this occurrence and one who seems to be afraid of it too, so back to you in the studio."

"Thank you, Sue Driscoll, our correspondent in London for that report. I suppose some of those views could represent how a lot of people are feeling about this right now."

"That's true Barbara, now just to allay fears of people about the attendance here of the President we understand that he has, in fact, ordered the Vice President Mr. Michael Jackson, the Secretary of Defense Tony Downe and all Joint Chiefs of Staff to move to secure locations at a range of sites including Cheyenne Mountain in case there is a situation developing here where he, himself, might be in some danger, so some precautionary measures being taken there to ensure that the processes of government will continue should a situation develop here for the worst. "

The CXN coverage continued to interview people in the street, with most expressing their grave concerns and fears but some expressing hopeful excitement.

"George we believe you have some more people standing by to express their view."

"Yes Barbara, I have here now a preacher from the Assembly of God Mr. James McPhee. James you seem to have a definite take on this situation?"

"Yes I believe that what we are seeing could well be the beginning of the end for us here on Earth, as foretold in the holy Bible, in the Book of Revelation - the Apocalypse - that the Lord will return at the end of times to save all true believers."

"Well perhaps it's best that we do not frighten too many people with that line already but, who knows, you might be right."

"Now finally, over here we have a couple who are obviously consoling each other somewhat so perhaps they can share their feelings."

The camera moved in on the couple who were kissing and suddenly startled by the interruption. They turned briefly toward the camera then immediately looked away and scurried off.

"Well it seems that perhaps they did not have anything to share with us."

For just a fleeting moment, Michael and Chrissy, who had ventured out together to check on the day's events, had let their guard down.

"Do you think we were just videoed by that television camera then?"

"Jesus! I hope not! I had better get home to Julie and the girls."

"Okay darling I will see you on Monday."

Michael went in one direction – Chrissy in the other.

Chapter 3

Back in the studio, things were about to turn in a different direction.

"Barbara, we have just received a call from Dr. Schubert Einstein who, of course, is very well known here in the United States and indeed right throughout the world as an eminent scientist who has been speculating for many years now about the possibility that intelligent life does exist elsewhere in the universe and we are just establishing a video link now with Dr. Einstein so that we can hear from him directly from the City University of New York. So perhaps we can cross live to Dr. Einstein now – Doctor Einstein, good morning and welcome to this live coverage from CXN of this most extraordinary event. A lot of people will be extremely interested to listen to you here this morning."

"Good morning Tom and good morning to you Barbara and Alex, I must say firstly that I am very excited by what I have been seeing here these last few minutes watching your coverage of this very strange and totally unexpected situation ... ah ... this really is quite a mind blowing experience for me."

"I would like to say first of all that I am not at all surprised by this occurrence as we have been speculating for quite some time now that intelligent civilizations may have been visiting the Earth for decades or even hundreds or thousands of years. In fact, the earliest known record of any person reporting a sighting of an unidentified flying object comes from China about the year 1088 when Shen Kuo in his "Dream Pool Essays" recorded that a flying object with windows and bright lights traveled at enormous speed across the sky. Prior to that, of course, there is some anecdotal evidence of extra-terrestrial visitations recorded in various art forms like rock paintings where strange objects resembling spaceships and astronauts were seemingly drawn by people in primitive societies."

"More recently there have been several very controversial reports of sightings since the late nineteenth and early twentieth centuries and especially since World War 11. Most people have heard of the Roswell incident and the "foo-fighters" from World War 11 and various other cases of 1946 and 1947 in the United States and many more in Scandinavian countries in Europe in the early 1940's."

"But, Dr. Einstein, how would this spacecraft get here to planet Earth, wherever it has come from, from anywhere else in the universe?"

"Well, Barbara, when you consider that our planet, the Earth, is about 4.5 billion years old and that we intelligent humans have evolved here from an ancestor that was very much ape-like, that of course being Australopithecus, over a period of just a few million years, it is entirely comprehensible that beings on other planets that are considerably older than the Earth - even within our own Milky Way galaxy - could have technology that is millions of years advanced on our own technology. In fact, when you consider that science has estimated that our own star, the Sun, has a life expectancy of another 5 billion years before it expands into a red giant and swallows up the Earth, it is conceivable that advanced civilizations could be, who knows, perhaps hundreds of millions of years more advanced than we are."

"So they must have cracked the code for space/time travel as we ourselves have been hypothesizing in for many years now in the hope that we can make the next big breakthrough, as we call it. Or they might have even come into our dimension or our universe from another dimension or another universe. That is something that astrophysicists have been debating for many years now, whether or not it is possible to travel faster than the speed of light. Or perhaps they have been able to traverse the universe by bending light to take some kind of short cut through space through wormholes or some other type of physical phenomenon, similar to what we saw in the "Stargate" movie."

"Having said that we must also ponder the possibility that whoever is visiting us here could actually be from another galaxy, perhaps the Andromeda galaxy or even a galaxy even more distant and when you consider that there are galaxies out there that may be several billions of years older than our own Milky Way, it is conceivable that the technology of these beings is billions of years ahead of our own. Of course, with the revelations from the Hubble telescope we now have a much better understanding of just how vast our universe is and how many galaxies and stars we are talking about here. The Hubble Deep Field view of 1995 and then the Hubble Extra Deep Field view of 2004 have completely blown us away because until then we had absolutely no idea that the universe is so concentrated with galaxies. Most of us within the scientific community had great difficulty comprehending the images that Hubble revealed, particularly with the Extreme Ultra Deep Field view because we could identify ten thousand galaxies in deep space a small area of the sky that is about the size of a grain of wheat held on your fingertip at arm's length."

"Then the Hubble Deep Field View South indicated to us that the universe looks the same in any direction, so we had to revise all estimates of the magnitude of the universe and its contents of galaxies and stars. So these visitors could be from a solar system that is considerably older than our own and perhaps they were where we are now, millions of years ago or even hundreds of millions of years ago. Can you imagine where our technology will be in one million years from now? So to them, Barbara, getting here to planet Earth could be like making a trip to the other side of the United States for a holiday."

"Yes and you have said just as much in your presentations on television that have become well known right throughout the world, Dr. Einstein, and for that I am sure that everybody will find some assurance in your confidence that this could be something very positive."

"Thank you Alex and I hope so, I hope that people all over the world who are watching this can rest assured that, as one young man from London said, any civilization that can traverse the universe is likely to have undergone a social evolution that would preclude them from any form of cataclysmic hostility, or war, as we know it only too well here on planet Earth. I don't think that we would ever be looking at a scenario similar to that portrayed in the film "Independence Day". Since the Second World War the nations of the world have taken strident steps towards peace through the United Nations and through international commerce and trade and recent events in the middle east give us hope that that process will continue. Whoever has come here today would have undergone quite a profound social evolution based on cooperation rather than conflict and they are probably very interested to study us the way an anthropologist would study a primitive society here on earth."

"Dr. Einstein, you said that coming here might be likened to a short holiday for them, do you think they might ... ah ... stay a while or would they need to return to their home planet, or even that this first contact might herald the arrival of many more spaceships from this civilization to our planet?"

"That's a very interesting question, Tom, obviously this visit could pave the way for many more – I suppose we just have to wait and see now what the initial dialogue with these people brings to light. They might have to report back to their leaders on what they have found here or the way we have responded to this and that may take some time because we just don't know yet how long it has taken them to travel here nor how far they have traveled to get here, but I am certainly very excited about finding some answers to those things. Who knows it may take a year or even longer for them to return to their home as it might for us to travel, say, to Mars and back to Earth. Perhaps they do this in a form of suspended animation as has been suggested in films like "Alien" where space travelers were in a state of deep freeze and were woken at a predetermined point of time by programmed computers. As for the possibility of them coming here en-masse, I think they will be very circumspect about the impact this first visitation will have on us here and of the possible level of disruption that would occur should large numbers of spaceships start arriving here on planet Earth."

"Yes Dr. Einstein I am very keen on your initial thoughts about the social impact of this event upon people all over the world ... ah ... just how do you think this is going to go down in different countries, different societies, indeed different cultures?"

"Well Barbara, I think one thing they will be totally cognizant of is the impact this will have on our religious belief systems. This visitation will come as quite a shock to billions of people all over the world who believe in God - be they Christians, Muslim, Hindu, Buddhist, Jewish or whatever. If their initial message to us indicates that they are friendly rather than hostile, that will go quite some way towards placating the substantial fear that might normally emanate from an event like this. I suppose the reaction - at least by some people - to the radio broadcast of War of the Worlds in the United States in October 1938 by Orson Welles is an indicator of how something like this could be received by a lot of people. We could have been looking at mass hysteria already but I believe they are civilized enough to understand this and I should imagine they will be quick to explain in more detail what their purpose is in coming here today. I hope and I do expect that they will be quick to assure people of all religious belief systems that their coming here does not undermine our belief systems."

"In fact this visitation may go quite some way toward giving us a far better understanding of the nature of God and I say that because of how my grandfather's cousin Albert Einstein felt about this. Einstein was completely blown away with humility just from contemplating the mind of God because he could understand and appreciate the mathematics of the universe and its order and majesty. To Einstein, God was discernible in the 'music' of the universe, as I have said in so many presentations, the universe could have been messy and chaotic rather than orderly and systematic. In fact, mathematicians who have worked on the rate of expansion of the universe have concluded that the rate of expansion is perfect for the universe to preserve itself – if the rate of expansion was any faster or slower the universe would not survive – it would either disintegrate or collapse upon itself and God got the number right on. So with their knowledge of the universe don't be at all surprised if these visitors here today can further our knowledge of the universe and hence move us closer to understanding the mind of God."

"Having said that I think it may be important for you good people at the CXN network to facilitate ... ah ... perhaps some form of communications with the leaders of the world's major religions, today."

"Yes that may be a good idea, Tom, Alex, what do you think, if we can set some wheels in motion straight away to, perhaps, allow for religious leaders here in the States or even from overseas to dial in via video link to us here at CXN to make some comment about the implications for their religious beliefs of what we are seeing here today."

"Sure, Barbara, I would be very pleased to hear what they would have to say about this."

"Yeah, me too! Dr. Einstein do you think the world's religious leaders could possibly explain this away somehow?"

"Well, just on that point Tom, I happen to know that Bob Lazar – who, of course, claims to have been privy to the so called Area 51 facility where alien craft have supposedly been stored - believes that the United States government gave total disclosure of the events of Roswell in 1947 to the Catholic Church in Rome at the time. If that is so then it seems to me that the Vatican has been dragging its feet on informing its people of the existence of alien life and of developing a doctrine that encompasses that within the Christian belief system, as if, the Vatican is afraid to go there. Perhaps the Vatican just did not know how to deal with the problem of alien life, as, you know, there were no explanations at that time of many fundamental tenets of the physical sciences as we know them today. Consider, for example, that with Hubble we now know just how vast the universe is and how old it is too, whereas, in 1947 there was still a considerable belief in creationism even within the Catholic Church. To the best of my knowledge it was Pope Pius XII who, in 1954 by virtue of Papal Encyclical, acceded that a process of evolution of species had taken place over millions of years and so started a re-education process within the Catholic clergy and its people. Even so, the sudden appearance of alien forms of life from other parts of the universe, at Roswell in 1947, must still have had the Catholic Church in quite a quandary for many years."

"What intrigues me about that assertion, Dr. Einstein, is, why would the U.S. Government confide such information in the Catholic Church, in particular, rather than other churches, considering that here in the United States, Catholics are outnumbered by non-Catholics by about two to one?"

"Well Alex, Catholic because you must remember that until Martin Luther posted his ninety-five theses on the door of the All Saints' Church in Wittenberg in October 1517, which virtually sparked the Protestant Reformation, the Catholic Church was *the* Christian church here on Earth. Martin Luther himself was a Catholic priest and monk until he was excommunicated by Pope Leo X for his recalcitrance, but also remember that Catholics are still the largest single denomination in The United States even today and were even more so back in 1947, so it was quite understandable that the U.S. Government would seek to confide in the church that has virtually been the bastion of Christian beliefs since the time of Jesus Christ.   Basically until 1517 there weren't any other Christian churches anywhere."

"Ah ... I didn't realize that, actually."

"Don't worry Alex a lot of people wouldn't. But remember also that the Catholic Church does trace its lineage back to the Apostles through the Papacy and, as such, represents the institutionalization of Christian beliefs, as distinct from Protestant Christian churches that may enjoy either prominence, or otherwise, at different times of their existence. So it would have been quite a natural gesture for the United States to divulge such information about the events at Roswell in 1947 to the church that represents the epitome of Christian churches here on Earth."

"Of course, Bob Lazar might be wrong, who knows, but some of the information he divulged to me about what he had supposedly witnessed at Area 51 and S4 certainly made me keep an open mind to it all. I was especially intrigued by what he referred to as element 115 that, when surrounded by an electromagnetic field, developed the property of negating gravity and of the supposed structure of the propulsion unit within the lower deck of the spacecraft that was, seemingly, comprised of three cylinders of this element that could be powered up to varying levels depending on how far one had to travel. He also referred to obvious differences in the nine craft that he supposedly observed and that he thought they might have come from the same place but from varying time locations, as if some were crude versions and some more advanced."

"Okay thank you Dr. Schubert Einstein we will keep you within reach as the day's events unfold here I am sure and we have taken your very good advice and have opened a line through our sub-editors here for any religious leaders who would like to call in via video link to let us know what their take is on this, so let's hope that we can get some words of reassurance here."

"Now, as we speak we have footage coming in of the Air Force jet that has flown the President from Washington to New York, together with five or six escort jets, touching down in a secluded zone of JFK airport, so we would expect that from there the President will have a police escort directly to the United Nations building where he has decided to hold a press conference."

"The time is 10:30am here in New York City, I am Tom Lowry, you are watching live coverage of this event on CXN News."

Chapter 4

The President arrives at the United Nations media room.

"Ladies and gentlemen, the President of the United States of America, Mr. Brett Bahama".

The applause is untypically subdued and truncated as there is an atmosphere of trepidation about the room. They have never confronted a situation like this before. What could the President possibly say to assure them that this is not some type of situation that is out of control? The room goes silent and the President looks around at the people there for several seconds before he begins to address them.

"Firstly, I want to appeal to everybody here and, indeed, everybody right throughout the United States of America to remain calm and to not panic as we are making every effort to analyze the situation at hand and we hope to ... ah ... bring you some updates on anything that we can ascertain about this unusual event. We already have a lot of people working on identifying what we are dealing with here and we are presently in communication with all administrations of all advanced countries and with the top people from Jane's, in an attempt to find out if this aircraft has been sent here from another country and, if so, where it might have come from and what purpose it could possibly serve in visiting us in this way and in ... ah ... infiltrating our airspace".

"There are several advanced countries that are more likely than others to have developed the scientific knowledge to achieve something like this - such as Russia, China, Germany, Britain and perhaps Japan too - but, if any of those countries have developed this kind of technology they have certainly kept us in the dark about it. Of course, just how they could manage to achieve that without keeping the world's scientific community informed about such technological developments would be rather perplexing to say the least."

"Now, I must hasten to add that if we do, in fact, find that no other advanced nation is responsible for this aircraft arriving here in New York City the way it has then ... ah ... I must appeal to everybody to just, have patience and to remain calm and to allow us to deal with whomsoever might be in control of this aircraft. It would be unwise to assume that this is a hostile situation regardless of where this aircraft is from."

"And also to pray to God for our safety."

"Mr. President, do you presently have any idea, whatsoever, of what this aircraft is or where it has come from?"

"At this point of time we do not actually have any information nor any knowledge of where this aircraft originated, but we are conducting analyses of scans taken by the Apache squadron and we hope to have some results within a matter of minutes now".

"Mr. President, is it at all possible this spaceship, is from somewhere here on Earth?"

"I wouldn't refer to this a spaceship at this point of time, but to answer your question, we are not ruling out any possibilities of that right now but, my intelligence services inform me that what we see here, in this aircraft that, obviously, has the ability to hover at a height and move so quickly, that we here in the United States are not aware of any known technology here on Earth that can currently do that sort of thing. If some other country has developed this type of technology, then, we do not yet know of it".

"Mr. President, are you considering any type of military response to this situation?"

"Given that we are still uncertain as to where this aircraft has come from or who is in control of it, or what they are doing here, any military response would be totally precipitant at this point of time. We here in the United States do not have a habit of shoot first and ask questions later - it is important to have some patience here and to be diplomatic and try to work with whomsoever is responsible to come to a resolution of this occurrence, depending on what it is that they want, of course."

"Apart from that, if this aircraft is what it seems to be, given that we do not have this technology, any military response would seem to be absolute folly, because, this aircraft is obviously from a very technologically advanced society, whether that be from eastern Europe or wherever. Given that their technology could also include advanced weaponry, we will not engage this aircraft with any form of hostility at this point of time."

"Mr. President just how soon do you expect to be briefed by your advisers to inform you of whether this aircraft does originate from somewhere on Earth - or whether we are dealing here with something from somewhere else?"

"As soon as I arrived here in New York I called for an update of whatever information they can provide me with, certainly within the hour, but also as information comes to hand. That information could be substantial, or it could be devoid of much detail, I don't really know at this point of time what they might be able to come up with."

"I would hasten to add, however that if this aircraft is from another nation here on Earth, we will be quick to demand some answers as to why this infiltration of our airspace has occurred without our prior knowledge, as we would regard this intrusion as a major transgression and, as such, as an act that could quite easily be regarded by us as a precursor to an act of war. So if some other nation is responsible they could find themselves in a lot of trouble right now."

Just as he spoke an adviser came into the room, approached the President and whispered into his ear – very reminiscent of the way an adviser had done to former President George W. Bush on September 11th 2001.

The adviser turned and walked away. The President looked around the room at all the people there, for several seconds, with a stunned look on his face. He seemed to be making an effort to summon the ability to speak. He took a deep breath.

"I ... have just been advised that our international liaison department within the Pentagon have been in contact with every known nation here on Earth that ... ah ... might have the ability to achieve something like this and, I have been informed that we are virtually one hundred per cent certain now that ... ah ... no other advanced nation here on Earth is responsible for this event."

Again he hesitated and looked around the room at the people with all eyes transfixed upon him.

"To quote one very famous line, it seems that the question of whether or not we are alone in the universe, has been answered."

There was an eerie silence about the room as people turned and looked at each other, with nobody really sure of what to say next, until one journalist broke the silence.

"Mr. President, you said that if you find that the aircraft is not from Earth then the people should pray to God for our safety. We know that you, sir, were raised into a Christian family within the Anglican Church. Don't you think that would be a good idea to pray to God now, regardless of where this aircraft is from?"

The President took another deep breath, nodded his head in concurrence with the journalist's suggestion, looked at the people around the room for a few seconds and, seeming rather emotional, he responded.

"I think it might be appropriate, actually, if we do pray to God together, now, so I ask you all to stand and, with me, to please recite The Lord's Prayer."

Everybody stood and, surprisingly, down to a person – even those who might normally be rather too inhibited to pray – they started to recite the Lord's Prayer together.

"Our Father who art in heaven
Hallowed be thy name
Thy kingdom come
Thy will be done on earth
As it is in heaven
Give us this day our daily bread
And forgive us our trespasses
As we forgive those who trespass against us
And lead us not into temptation
But deliver us from evil
For thine is the kingdom, the power and the glory

Forever and ever. Amen."

Just as they completed the Lord's Prayer the adviser came back into the room and again whispered into the President's ear.

The President looked at the people in the room and made a statement.

"I have just been informed that there is a development of some kind taking place at the moment and we should view this on the screen here."

An aide pointed a controller at the screen and clicked the button to bring the CXN coverage into the room. The reporter in the CXN media room had just crossed back to the reporter in the helicopter. They picked up the coverage midway through a comment.

"... so now four of the five windows on this side of this aircraft have just turned from that almost black color, to white ... and now the fifth window is also turning white ... so all five windows on this side of this aircraft have just changed appearance from that black color they had before to a bright white color."

"Rod does it look as though this could be an attack or perhaps they are preparing for something sinister?"

"That's just too difficult to say right now, Barbara ... ah ... golly, all we can see at the moment is that the aircraft is still hovering where it has been for the last two hours, but that the five windows on the front of the aircraft have changed color from black to white. The four Apache choppers are still in position surrounding this aircraft and, obviously, would be on red alert to respond if anything sinister were to occur."

People in the media room became restless, turning to each other and seeking assurance from each other, asking what others were thinking about this change in the appearance of the spaceship, until somebody spoke up to ask the President.

"Mr. President, what do you make of this change, do you think this could signal that the occupants of this spaceship are about to do something here?"

"I'm sorry ... I honestly have no idea."

Then the reporter in the helicopter spoke up again.

"We certainly hope that whatever is happening here now is not ... ah ... something to be afraid of ... wait a minute, now, something else is happening here, we see a change occurring in window five – it looks like some type of symbol developing here as part of this window is changing color there seems to be some blackness coming back into this window and now, we ... we see a symbol that resembles the letter "e" in window five and now window four is changing too ... ah ... we see a symbol here that is developing and it seems to be the letter "c" and now the other windows, too, are changing to partially black ... ah ... we see perhaps a letter "a" in window three and now another "e" in window two and now – oh my God, oh my God – would you look at that. Do you believe that?"

He turned to the camera and beamed a wide smile.

"They have just written the letter "p" in window one and have spelt out the word "peace" here in these five windows. Do you believe this?"

There was an outburst of spontaneous cheering, applause and laughter in the media room as people turned to each other and with overwhelming joy began to embrace and hug and kiss each other. People were shaking hands and patting each other on the shoulders and some women were screaming with joy. The President, too, was looking around the room at everybody there with an enormous smile on his face, his aides were shaking his hand, they were nodding their heads and looking back at the screen where the spaceship was still the focus of the cameras, though nobody in the room could hear any of the reporters at that time.

The President placed his left hand over his mouth for

several seconds, obviously with enormous relief as he looked back at the screen, nodding his head with approval, then he looked back at the people in the room and held both his hands upwards towards the ceiling before he joined his hands together in front of his mouth, much the same way as he done as a young man many years before in a prayerful posture in church. There was still a substantial din in the room so he raised both his hands above his head to signal to everybody to pay attention to him.

As people in the room brought others to attention the din faded into silence as everybody waited to hear the President speak again.

As the television coverage had momentarily been rendered rather superfluous an aide turned down the volume to allow the President to speak.

"My dear people" as he looked around the room nodding his head with a rather relieved smile across his face, "it seems to me that perhaps our prayers have already been answered and ... ah ... I would like you all to be with me now as I say a very special prayer, in thanking our God for this early sign that, hopefully, we may have nothing to fear from this event."

He clasped his hands together again. "Our Father who art in heaven" he paused for a deep breath, "my Lord Jesus Christ" he paused again, "Holy Spirit of God. We thank you dear God, we thank you dear God, we thank you dear God, for this sign of reassurance here this morning, that we may not be in any form of peril from whomsoever is occupying this very strange aircraft that has visited us here today. We join together in asking Lord, that our prayers and our hopes are not in vain."

At this there was a collective "amen" as the Presidential aide then proceeded to return some volume to the television coverage. Again, they picked up on the commentary mid-sentence.

"... that they have the technology to understand our language and are able to communicate with us in this way."

Barbara Foster turns back towards the camera to address the viewers again.

"Just repeating the news of this latest occurrence now, for the sake of all people right throughout the world who are watching these events unfold here in New York City, we can tell you that whoever is in control of this very strange aircraft that is hovering above the United Nations building that, on the surface of it, appears to be an unidentified flying object or spacecraft of some kind, has just spelt out the word "peace" in the five windows that adorn the side of the aircraft. So let us cross back now live to our on the ground reporter at the scene George Bowman. George, what is the reaction of people there right now?"

"Barbara, I can tell you there was instantaneous jubilation here as soon as the large screen here lit up that word "peace" ... ah ... everybody started cheering and clapping and raising their hands to the sky and waving their arms above their heads. There were people here kissing and hugging each other and laughing – it was a very, very chilling experience I can tell you. I have never experienced anything remotely like this ever before. I am just going to ask a young lady here what her thoughts are about this. Excuse me miss, can you tell me what you are thinking right now?"

"Wow, I am just so relieved, I was just hoping and praying that these people would turn out to be friendly and I, kinda, knew that for an alien race to come here from somewhere else in the galaxy they would probably have to be friendly, because, you know, I just don't think that any civilization that is hostile is going to survive long enough to be able to do this, you know."

Her friend interjected!

"Yeah man, I knew it too - if they were hostile among

themselves and had this type of technology, they would have destroyed themselves long before they came here man."

"So let us cross back now live to our reporter in London Sue Driscoll to see the reaction over there in London. Sue what can you tell us about this now, have people there taken this in yet?"

"Barbara, there is a situation here like I have never seen before – it is like everybody is so totally jubilant and everybody is moving around smiling and laughing. Men are shaking hands and embracing each other, women are kissing and hugging each other, men are kissing women – I have never seen anything like this. I suppose there is a tremendous release of relief here because, needless to say, a lot of folks here were genuinely worried about this situation in New York, after what happened in September 2001. Let me just ask a young man here now who seems rather calm about it all what he thinks about this. Excuse me sir, would you mind sharing how you feel about this please?"

"I don't know ... I just hope this is for real. It will be great if this is but I just hope this is not some kind of a trick, you know."

"Well let's all hope so! Barbara, Tom, Alex, it's back to you in New York."

"Thank you Sue Driscoll our correspondent there in London reporting from Trafalgar Square. I suppose there could be a lot of people all over the world right now feeling the same sentiments expressed by that young man in London, just hoping ..."

"And praying!"

"Yes indeed Alex, praying too, that this initial message of peace that our visitors – whoever they may be – have displayed in their five windows here is not some kind of a subterfuge, or trickery. Let's all just hope and pray that this is a genuine message from them. But where do we go from here?"

Back in the media room the President gave his closest aide an instruction.

"I want you to inform the Chief of Defense that I would like the Apache helicopters to back away from the immediate vicinity right now so as to not antagonize whoever is visiting us here today."

"With respect Sir, I am not sure that is such a good idea at this point of time ..."

"Now!"

"Ah ... yes Sir!"

"Ralph! It will be a very important gesture for our people too, okay – go some way toward attenuating their concern and placating them at this point of time, which they may need right now. Just get the choppers to back off about a half mile or so. Okay?"

"Ah ... yes Sir! Understood Sir! What happens then, Sir?"

"We probably need to leave the next move up to them. We'll just have to wait and see."

The senior aide passed the order down the line and it was very quickly passed on to the chopper pilots. As the Apache choppers turned away from the spaceship and took up a position almost one mile away, the CXN reporter Rod Saunders found himself and his crew as the only remaining aircraft in the vicinity. Understandably, he continued his report with just a trace of malaise evident in his voice.

"Ah ... something is happening here, Barbara, one of the Apache helicopters has done a turn and is starting to move away from the spaceship, no, wait, the other Apache's too are turning now and ... ah ... we are still here as we have not been ordered to leave the area. It seems that someone has given the order for the Air Force Apache's to leave. They were in position just about one hundred yards away from the spaceship and we are still here just five hundred yards away, but the Apache's are retreating. I can see them now hovering in the distance perhaps about a half mile or more away from here. So we are now the only aircraft in this immediate vicinity and I really have no idea what is going to happen next but we are going to stay right here and cover this story until someone tells us to do otherwise. So for now, Barbara, Alex, Tom, it's back to you in the studio."

Chapter 5

Attention then turned back to the CXN studio.

"Okay we have just received word from our correspondent within the Pentagon that the President did, in fact, order the Air Force to retreat from the immediate area for now, hoping that this will convey a message of acceptance of the "peace" gesture that the occupants of this spaceship have offered to us and hoping to educe some kind of further response from them. What that might be is, of course, anybody's guess. I am not exactly sure what the President might be hoping for next."

You are watching CXN's live coverage of this most unusual event here in New York City of what appears to be an Unidentified Flying Object hovering above the United Nations building. We have just opened our video conferencing lines for any of the nation's religious leaders to ..."

"Hold fire on that one guys, something is happening here now. From our position here in the CXN chopper we see that the spaceship has descended from where it was about fifty feet above the top of the building down to just about maybe, just four feet if that. Now it looks as though a small doorway has opened beneath this spaceship and ... ah ... the door itself has been lowered and then extended toward the rooftop of the United Nations building as though it is to form a stairway for someone to exit this thing. So we have some action going on here."

"Rod is there any sign of movement from within or any sign of life at all?"

"Not yet but this looks all set now for someone to come out of this spacecraft and on to the roof of the UN building."

"Ralph, Lynda, I want you to come with me to the rooftop. We will go up through the conference room above here and greet whoever is about to exit this spaceship."

"Mr. President I strongly advise that you at least take some armed men with you sir."

"Okay but just two or three, we don't want to alarm these ... whoever they might be."

The President turned to address the media people that he would make his best endeavors to return as soon as possible to let them know where this spaceship had come from and why they were here. Then he and his two closest aides and three armed aides made their way to the rooftop. Upon their arrival there they were able to see, first-hand, that the spaceship had an open door and a gangway leading down to the rooftop. They stepped forward to a position about ten yards from the spaceship. There was a dim haze of blue light within the craft. Then they noticed some movement within the spaceship. This was a moment of high anxiety for all of them, the very first verifiable encounter of human beings with aliens. They all just stood there staring, not knowing what to expect next. The President felt that Neil Armstrong must have been feeling the same way before he set foot on the moon. Ralph, Lynda and the two aides were all feeling a sense of malaise and their hearts and their minds were racing.

Then, just within the doorway of the spaceship there appeared some slight movement and a distinct color of red. Then to the right the color green appeared and to the left the color blue. Then the colors started to move. It soon became evident that three small beings wearing these colors were moving within the spaceship – and moving toward the doorway. With each passing second, they became a little clearer, until they had all appeared at the doorway, where they stopped for a few moments, looking at the President and his entourage of five. There they were – three alien beings each about four feet in height wearing the most striking ruby red, emerald green and sapphire blue cape or gown, rather similar to a priest's chasuble, but with a thick yellow collar wrapped around the neck. Their eyes were large and black. Essentially, they bore a very strong resemblance to the classical alien appearance as outlined by so many people who had claimed encounters with aliens. All three of them were holding a small item in their hands.

"Would you look at this – we can now see three small alien type figures standing in the doorway of this spaceship ... ah ... the one at the front is wearing red and there are two behind him, one dressed in green and the other in blue. They seem to be quite short and they do have those large black almond shaped eyes that slant upwards just the way that people have been saying for so long."

"Rod those really are amazing pictures you are sending us now but is there any way you guys can either zoom in closer on this or even move a little closer for us?"

"Well Barbara, we are still the only ones here and still no one has told us to steer clear so, yeah, we will move closer and get a better take on this."

He doesn't know what prompted him to do it but, as the three aliens were standing at the doorway of their spaceship, the President decided that he would bow his head in deference to the visitors. His aides all followed his lead, with the President looking down for a few seconds before looking up again, only to see the aliens do exactly the same. Now they all felt a lot easier. The President then extended both his arms forward with his hands open as if to welcome the visitors.

He seemed to know what he was doing, for at this the leading visitor took a step forward and his two followers did the same. The President then motioned with his hands for them to come forward. With seemingly a little trepidation, the visitors then took their first tentative steps onto planet Earth. When they reached the bottom of the gangway and stepped onto the rooftop, the President motioned with his hands for them to come forward towards the rooftop service room. They walked forward a little clumsily, as if stepping off a plane after a long flight.

"Would you take a look at that – those three small aliens have now stepped out of the doorway of this spaceship and have stepped onto the rooftop of the building and it seems as though the President has … ah … invited them into the building. The one at the front wearing red seems to be the leader and the two behind him, one dressed in green and the other in blue are just a couple of feet behind him. They all seem to be carrying a small item in their hands, rather reminiscent to me of the three wise men who bore gifts to the infant Jesus. Now they are going through the doorway and into the building and still the spaceship just hovers there. Barbara, it's back to you!"

"Absolutely extraordinary scenes there as three alien beings have quite openly arrived here in New York City and have left their spaceship to perhaps, enter some form of dialogue with the President of the United States, who, you could see there was quite forthcoming in the way he welcomed them and that, too, really is quite extraordinary that a man of his position would be there himself, in person, right at the front of all the action here. That really is amazing. Thank God for our President!"

"Yes, Barbara, that is quite true, even though he did have four or five aides close by and probably some of them armed, too, I should think, but what an absolutely amazing gesture of goodwill toward our very first alien visitors for the President of the United States to personally be there to welcome them to our planet Earth."

"I'm wondering what happens next - wherever they are, will they be able to communicate?"

"Well, Tom, we did see them spell out the word "peace" for us so let's just hope that they do have some means of communication with us. I should think they would have. Now we have just been informed by our people in the media room that the President gave an undertaking that he would be back as soon as he could be to let us all know who these visitors are, where they come from and what they are doing here, so let's all hope that he can do that soon."

"Now as suggested by Dr. Einstein, we made a call just before the aliens came out of their spaceship, for religious leaders to come forward to give their take on this event and we have our first video link happening here with ... ah ... Pastor Nathan Knorr the Fourth of the Jehovah's Witnesses right here in Brooklyn on-line now. Pastor Knorr good morning to you, thank you for your time here today ... ah ... please tell us what you make of this very strange situation."

"Good morning Barbara, Alex, Tom and good morning to all of your viewers. Basically, I think that what we are seeing here is something that was predicted by our founder so long ago, that is the imminent return of Jesus Christ to rule over the world as has been foretold in the sacred scriptures and espoused by us ever since our society was formed late in the nineteenth century by Pastor Charles Taze Russell."

"Pastor Russell was a founder of the Watchtower Bible and Tract Society of Pennsylvania and predicted as early as 1877 that the world would come to an end in 1914 with the return of Jesus Christ to rule over the world and ... ah ... when this seemingly did not happen Pastor Russell realized that the true date could be sometime in 1916. Then, fortunately, shortly before his death in October 1916 Pastor Russell came to the realization that the return of Jesus Christ did, in fact, occur in accordance with his first prediction in October 1914 but that this occurred in the upper air."

"We believe that what we are seeing here today could be the culmination of Pastor Russell's original prediction about the end of times and that this chariot that is hovering over the United Nations building has brought Abraham, Moses and Elijah back to the Earth to prepare for the return of Jesus, to form Jehovah's government here on Earth and that all of our people will be going either to heaven or to paradise, today. This is fundamental to all our beliefs and I am very excited about this because Jehovah's Witnesses all over the world have been waiting for this for a long, long time now. Our people all over the world should be very excited about this. I must add that we believe this day will bring an end to all man-made governments everywhere around the world ..."

"Excuse me Pastor Knorr, you have said that this day all of your people will either be going to Heaven or to paradise, do you actually mean that heaven and paradise are one and the same place or are you referring to ... ah ... two different places here?"

"I refer to heaven as the spiritual place where one hundred and forty-four thousands of our people will live forever in the presence of God, as this is the number referred to in the holy scriptures as being the twelve tribes of Israel and all other Jehovah's Witnesses will live in paradise governed by God's government where they will enjoy all things and all needs will be met. They will have all the food they need, they will live together in total harmony with all of the animals of the earth and they will not have to work ever again. This is the promise that our founder and other great men like Pastor Rutherford and my own great grandfather foretold so long ago and we knew this would happen one day. And to all the people who have not believed us and who are now finding out it is too late they are just gonna have to suck it up!"

"Pastor Knorr you paint a very idyllic picture there and many of us would be quite familiar with this utopian existence that your church assures your own people that they are going to enjoy forever at the exclusion of everybody else, but there is one thing I would like to clarify while you are here."

"Yes and what is that?"

"Well I do have a small confession to make - your people knocked on my front door recently and I was in such a hurry to leave my house that I thought the best way to see them off was to buy the Watchtower and the Awake which they were very happy to sell to me. I did manage to read some of it on the train. Now it just seems to me that what is written within both publications would appeal to people of a rather low intellect and I pondered the drawings of this idyllic life being surrounded by animals like lions and gazelles and also by plentiful fruit like bananas and pineapples and things. Well I just couldn't help wondering if the people reading these magazines really believe that in this paradise the lions will be vegetarian."

"Alex, the Lord will provide for the lions in his own way, just as he did with the loaves and fishes with which he was able to feed over five thousand people. So the lions will be taken good care of, you don't need to worry about that. There will be no violence in the paradise the Lord has reserved for all Jehovah's people."

"And what will become of everybody else – all of the people who are not part of your church, Pastor Knorr?"

"All other persons - that is all persons who are not Jehovah's Witnesses - will not be given a place in heaven nor in paradise."

"So you are talking about all other Christians such as Baptist and Church of Christ and Assembly of God and Catholic and Muslim people too?"

"Yes! Of course!"

"So what will become of them if they are not going to heaven or paradise?"

"They will be sent to their grave and they will simply cease to exist."

The video started to 'blink' a little.

"Well that's what they told me once when I did listen to them but I wasn't really sure whether to believe it, so that is what you believe, so let's all hope that you are not right.

Pastor Knorr thank you for appearing here this morning on CXN."

"Ah ... okay, we might just leave it at that for the moment, we seem to have a slight technical problem with that video link, Pastor Knorr of the Jehovah's Witnesses here in Brooklyn, thank you for your time. We may try to get him back here if we can just re-establish that link, later."

"Guys! Any comment about that?"

"Oh I think that most people would be quite familiar with the views of the Jehovah's Witnesses on this ... ah ... most of us have had them knock on our door sometime and peddle their beliefs with their magazines and their lines of discussion, or argument. What Pastor Knorr had to say there before we lost him is entirely in accordance with what they believe - that Jehovah God will send his son Jesus Christ back to Earth and that he will form God's government here and that all other governments, along with everybody who is not a Jehovah's Witness will, basically, perish."

"Yes and they believe that Jesus Christ was a prophet and the son of God, but not God, is that correct?"

"Yes that's true, Tom, they do not believe in the concept of the Trinity as being three persons in one God - Father, Son and Holy Spirit - as most other Christian religions do."

"We now have a second caller on video link and this is Mr. Tim Krause on-line from the Church of Scientology, good morning Tim."

"Good morning Alex, Barbara, Tom and good morning to all people in America, I have got to say, firstly, that I am not ... ah ... we are not surprised by this event either because we believe that all human beings are immortal aliens, a spiritual

66

being, that is trapped on planet Earth in a physical body. We call our alien spirit a 'thetan' and we do believe that the human race was actually placed here on the planet Earth by an alien race of thetans, so what we see happening here today is not something for us within the Church of Scientology to be afraid of, at all. In fact what is occurring gels quite comfortably with what we have been teaching for many decades now ever since L. Ron Hubbard developed his teaching. We have always believed that the thetans might actually return to Earth at some point of time in the future to provide us with additional guidance or to give us now directions to move in. Some within our church even believe that the thetans will come here to take us back home when we have reached a certain point of enlightenment."

"Ah ... isn't that something like what the Hale-Bopp people believed way back in – when was it – 1998?"

"We would actually take quite some umbrage, Tom Lowry, to being compared in any way whatsoever to the Heaven's Gate people who took their lives back in 1997, the year was Tom. You know that kind of comment just is not going to help anybody here, you know what I mean, Tom Lowry? Do you get the message?"

"Well if the hat fits, wear it Tim. I'm sure you will find that your average, every day, rational-thinking, common sense American just would not buy into that kind of stuff – that we have all been planted here by aliens. You know what I mean, Tim Krause?"

"Well look at what is happening right there in front of your own short-sighted eyes, Tom Lowry, there is an alien spacecraft atop the United Nations building and as we speak they are in dialogue with the President of the United States. Now your average, every day, rational-thinking, common sense American may not have believed that this was going to happen either at about eight a.m. this morning when they left for work, so Tom Lowry, just pull your head in because there are obviously some alien people right here and now, you know."

"Yes and it still remains to be seen who they are, where they have come from and what they are doing here and at this point of time they have not suggested to anybody that they planted us people here on Earth either. So Tim Krause, thank you for your time here this morning on CXN."

"Well I haven't actually finished yet ... Barbara Foster, would you mind if I direct my address through you please rather than through Mr. Tom Lowry?"

"We might just get back to you later on that Tim if you don't mind. We need to cross now to another religious leader who has been quick to contact us here today on CXN. We have Mr. Kenneth Pokeland and his wife Georgia of Pokeland Ministries on-line now. Kenneth and Georgia, good morning and thank you for calling in, please tell us how you think the Assembly of God churches here in the States are receiving this now."

"Well by golly I gotta tell ya that we believe this may well be the second coming of our Lord Jesus Christ right here, amen. The book of Revelation, I say, the book of Revelation says that the Lord is gonna come again in glory, and victory will be his, praise be to God, alleluia. That sure does look like a mighty fine aircraft he got there don't it? I wouldn't mind, I say, I wouldn't mind having one of them on my runway too I tell ya."

"Yes we believe that you do, in fact, have your own runway on the ranch, but what do you think about these aliens who have come here today?"

"Aliens?"

"Yes, three of them stepped out of this spaceship not so long ago and are presently in dialogue with the President of the United States at the top of the United Nations building. If this is the second coming of Jesus Christ who do you think these three aliens might be?"

"Well I would have to say that I might just agree with your earlier guest who suggested that the three people we saw could be Abraham, Moses and Elijah, I say, don't forget that they were all present at the transfiguration of our Lord Jesus Christ atop a mountain before he rode to victory into Jerusalem. So I do believe they may be preparing the way for the Lord."

"So do you think that the Lord Jesus Christ might be waiting inside the spaceship?"

"By golly no, he wouldn't be in there he would be coming after they have prepared the way for the Lord which is probably what they are doing there with the President right now. No the Lord, I say, the Lord would be on his way at a time of his choosing which could be today or it could be tomorrow or even next week. There could be quite some preparation to be taken care of here. Why the Lord just might want to give a lot of good folks a chance to take heed of this warning and to convert in these next few days so that they can be saved."

"And how do people do that?"

"They best get on down to their local congregation of the Assembly of God and join up, or, for anybody who wants to be converted right here and now and to enter eternal life in heaven I would ask them to close their eyes and join their hands together and to pray this prayer with me now."

He closed his eyes to pray.

"My dear Lord God I come before you today as a sinner, I know I have done wrong dear God and I am truly sorry for all of my sins and I repent today dear Lord God from all of my evil ways and I promise I will never sin again and I accept the Lord Jesus Christ as my personal Lord and savior and I give my life to you oh Lord and I ask you to baptize me with the Holy Spirit. In Jesus' name. Amen"

He opened his eyes.

"By golly!"

"Are you sure that's all it takes?"

"If you pray that prayer, which you can find at our website pokelandministries.com and you are baptized with the Holy Spirit of God then you have been born again and you will gain eternal life. Then you can raise your voice to God and give your voice over to God to allow him to pray for you through the Holy Spirit - in tongues."

"In tongues?"

"Just as the Apostles did after Jesus' ascension into Heaven. They went forth and preached the gospel to all people everywhere in their own native language because they had received the gift of tongues and everybody was able to understand what they were saying."

"A lot of people may not have time to get to their local Assembly of God branch depending on what happens here today, so they would be best advised to visit your website then."

"That may be the best thing to do in current circumstances, I gotta tell ya, so you have, I say, you have the website address, now when you get there you can all join up online, because we have credit card facilities so you can use your Visa card or your American Express or even Paypal to become a member of our church today."

"Why would they need to pay anything?"

"Because the Lord, Tom Lowry, wants his people to give a tithe as evidence of their faith in God and their commitment to that faith, so our people give a tithing to the church."

"And this tithing is a tenth of their income?"

"It is yes and if you have never been a tither and you are worried that the Lord might hold this against you, well I gotta tell ya that that just might be the case now, so if you want to make up for lost ground and become a retrospective tither, I would suggest that you deposit ten percent of what you would have given over so many years, perhaps even ten percent of what your net worth is right here, 'cos that way the Lord, I say, the Lord is gonna look upon you far more favorably now."

"Now you non tithers, you think the Lord is going to be standing there at those pearly gates just a waitin' for ya? Well I gotta tell ya, I say, I gotta tell ya that just ain't gonna happen, so you best get to our website now and sign in to become a tither because it ain't never too late."

"Thank you for that Mr. Ken Pokeland, now we have another of your fellow Assembly of God ministers coming on-line now ... ah ... I believe this is James Robertson appearing on our second video link screen here. We will keep Kenneth online too now. Good morning James, thank you for calling in on this momentous occasion. We have just heard from your fellow pastor Kenneth Pokeland who is still online here and has given our viewers the benefit of a prayer that he invited them to share with him and he has advised people that they can become a church member through his website."

"Well just allow me to reiterate something that Kenneth touched on right there, you know Jesus said that no-one can enter the kingdom of heaven unless he is born again and we here at the Assembly of God we do believe in the Bible. So any folks who are afraid of what they are seeing here today and might be worried about the fate of their eternal soul need to turn to God today because it's not too late. In fact with the Lord it's never too late, you know, because he gave us the parable of the vineyard owner who put people out to work in the early morning and then some in the middle of the day and then some near the end of the day and at the end of the day they all received the same reward. Jesus also said that no-one goes to the Father except through me. So any folks who want to pray a prayer that can save their souls today could go to our website robertsonministries.com and become a believer today because this just might be the final judgement day right here."

"Well Kenneth has invited people to visit his website and to pray the prayer that he gave us earlier ..."

"We have a very similar prayer at our website that will also turn people to God because it is just so important that they repent here today and give their lives over to the Lord and to become a believer in Jesus Christ as the Son of God and in doing this they will be born again and be able to return to the Father just as Jesus said, through him."

"And they would need to become a member of the church by making some kind of a pledge of about ten percent of what they earn each week, is that right James?"

"Yes sir, Alex, they can do that via our website because we also have all of the credit card facilities available right there ..."

"They already have details of how to become a tither at our website at Pokelandministries where they can do all of that James ..."

"Well I'm just a little worried that your website might crash Kenneth, if you get a few million people all trying to access your website at the same time now ..."

"No look we have been assured by our webmaster that our site can join up millions and millions of people ..."

"But not all at the same time and you wouldn't want any souls to be lost now, simply because they could not become a believer in Jesus Christ because your website is too busy now, would you?"

"Well I did come along here before you did now!"

"Gentlemen it seems that we may have Mr. Creflo Dollar coming through on a third line now ..."

"Alex I think it would be best if we just stay with these two gentlemen for now, we might see if Mr. Dollar can possibly call back later ..."

Barbara Foster looks toward a studio technician endeavoring to catch her attention.

"And Jesse Duplantis too, now, okay. I beg your pardon?"

"And now Marilyn Hickey also, okay. Well we just might have to place those three on hold for now and possibly call upon them later should we need to."

"Okay Barbara thank you, now gentlemen, can we just bring this back to where we should be now … ah … where were we a few minutes ago?"

"We were talking about the prayer actually."

"Thank you Barbara, now while you are both here you have mentioned the prayer that people should pray to give their lives to the Lord and with this they will be born again and that this is a requirement for salvation."

"Yes they will be baptized with the Holy Spirit."

"And to become a tither!"

"And to pray in tongues!"

"Ah yes, that's where we were, I recall you saying that earlier Kenneth. You said that people should give their voice over to God and that they need to pray in tongues."

"Well … yeah … that is the evidence that they have been baptized with the Holy Spirit. In Jesus' name, amen!"

"I'm not really sure that I follow this Kenneth, does that mean that people who go to your website and pray this special prayer that they can find there are going to somehow pick up a new language here?"

"They need to give their voice over to the Lord and to just start making a little noise and just let the good Lord take their voice wherever he wants to take it, you hear?"

"James?"

"The person praying in tongues may not understand what they are praying but they will be praying whatever their soul needs to pray for them at that time. It is like, the perfect prayer for that soul at that time."

"Thank you for that James, but does that mean they will be praying in Greek or Italian or Spanish or what?"

"Well no Alex, they will be praying in a language that the Holy Spirit understands and it will be coming from the depths of their soul. Whatever their soul needs to pray at that time."

"And you say that this, too, is a requirement to be saved."

"The gift of tongues is evidence that a person is born again, yes."

"So the people praying this prayer in tongues won't actually understand what they are praying."

"Well that's right but somebody else, I say, somebody else might!"

"Not really sure that I follow you on that Georgia, what do you mean by that?"

"Well when people are baptized with the Holy Spirit they receive all kinds of gifts, you know and ... ah ... some people receive the gift of interpretation of tongues, so if you were with somebody who was praying in tongues even though they might not actually know what they are praying, you might be able to interpret what they are praying. We see this all the time at our services, where somebody will be moved to pray in tongues and somebody else will provide the interpretation."

"So could you two demonstrate this to us here now so that people watching this might glean from this a better understanding of what you mean?"

"Well praying in tongues is a rather personal thing, you know, we should remember that Jesus said to go to your room and pray in private. But if somebody was to pray in tongues before you now an interpreter might say, for example ... ah ... 'I am with you my sons, I will show you the way, I will bless the ground where you walk' and so that might be the true meaning of what was prayed in tongues."

"Okay well, just finally, James if people were to visit your website and become a member of your church today, how much do you think they would need to contribute to be saved?"

"There's no set amount on this, it's basically up to each person to perhaps decide whether or not they want to become a tither or whether they can only give so much now and perhaps become a tither later."

"Kenneth?"

"Now I gotta tell ya, if you think the Lord wants to wrench your hand open to get your tithings, no, by golly he wants you to give freely. Don't be afraid now to part with what you got 'ços you can't take it with you when you go and you gonna spend a long time, I say, a long time in eternity wherever you goin' to. In Jesus' name, amen!"

"If this is the second coming of Jesus Christ and the world is about to come to an end, why would you want people to hand over ten percent of everything they own? What are you going to do with all that money? Are you going to take it to heaven when you go there?"

"No Alex we are not, I say, we are not going to take any money anywhere when the Lord cometh and the point is that nobody else can either. What is important about this is that people now have an opportunity to be saved right here for all eternity and this requires people to turn away from their sinfulness and to repent and to believe in Jesus Christ as their own personal Lord and savior and to be baptized in the Holy Spirit so they may be born again and to pray in tongues and to become a tither. That is all it takes and the giving of the ten percent, even though it ain't gonna go nowhere if the world ends right here, it would be symbolic that they had turned to God in these last days."

"Okay, Kenneth, James, thank you for your time here this morning on CXN, let's all hope that people out there have made sense of all of that, somehow."

"It seems that we have another senior minister on the line now, this is Mr. Rick Measle from the Bible Discernment Ministry, good morning to you Rick."

"Good morning to all you good folk at CXN and to all true believers of the true church of God."

"Rick, can you please tell us how your church is feeling about this UFO that has come here today."

"We believe that this could be the work of Satan. We believe that God created an innumerable company of spiritual beings, known as angels and that one, Lucifer, the highest in rank, sinned through pride, and thereby became Satan. We believe that a great company of the angels followed him in his moral fall, that some became demons and are active as his agents and associates in the prosecution of his unholy purposes and that others who fell are reserved in everlasting chains under darkness unto the judgment of the great day."

"Ah ... Rick, do you share any of the views of the ministers who have already expressed their thoughts here this morning?"

"We are opposed to all forms of theological compromise, apostasy, liberalism, modernism, ecumenical evangelism, neo-orthodoxy, neo-evangelicalism and the charismatic and ecumenical movements of our day. We believe that all are out of harmony with the Word of God and the official doctrine and position of the Bible Discernment Ministry and are inimical to the Word of God. Since we believe that evil, false doctrine and spiritual compromise are all contagious, we thereby believe that the only way the purity, peace, and reputation of the church can be maintained is by separation - both personal and ecclesiastical. Christians are to be in the world, but not of it, having no friendship, affiliation, nor identification with it. Likewise, Christians should not attempt to 'Christianize' the world's principles and practices and bring them into the Church as part of Christian worship, fellowship, prayer, preaching, or communion. We also believe in the separation from detractors of orthodox doctrine - unbiblical ecclesiastical practices - that is, neo-evangelicalism, ecumenism, ecclesiastical apostasy, modernism/liberalism, and the charismatic movement, immoral unrepentant 'believers', and the state. Moreover, we believe that Christians are commanded by Scripture to withdraw from professing brethren who enter into memberships, affiliations, and fellowships including evangelistic crusades, youth movements, mission agencies, schools, etcetera which seek to unite separatist fundamentalists with those who do not obey the Biblical teachings on separation, that is, with those who refuse to obey the Biblical doctrine of separation."

"Ah ... Rick, we may not have a lot of time to go into such doctrine at great length here this morning but it seems that you are saying that you do not have a lot in common with our previous guests, or perhaps anybody else for that matter and I am sure if any viewers wish to learn more about anything you have said they can visit your website too. Rick Measle, we do thank you for calling in."

"Now we are still awaiting the return of the President from his initial meeting with our visitor friends, as we should call them and hopefully when he does come out he brings some comforting news to his American citizens and, indeed, to all people all over the world who are watching us here on CXN."

Chapter 6

Back on top of the United Nations building, once the three aliens had entered the rooftop conference room they just stood there for a short time rather motionless, holding their three items, as if waiting for someone to do something. Then the leader of the aliens extended his arms, holding the item he was carrying out toward the President. The President stepped forward and received the item from the alien leader and, acknowledging that he was being presented with a gift of some kind, bowed his head in gratefulness. This seemed to be a gesture they understood for the aliens, too, bowed their heads toward the President. The item was a small metallic box that seemed to contain a few small holes and a black lens on one side.

The President turned and motioned for an aide to work out what to do with this gift. He fetched a small table from the corner of the room and the President placed the item onto the table. What happened next astonished everybody - a voice came from within the box - a beautiful, female voice.

"Greetings to you Mr. President - and to the people of your world!"

Everybody in the room looked around at each other and at the aliens with some surprise, for none of the aliens had appeared to speak.

"Do not be concerned nor alarmed for we do come to you in peace. I am able to communicate directly with you, in your own language, with our gift as we have complete knowledge of your communication systems. We, ourselves, no longer speak physically but communicate with each other only through mental telepathy. My thoughts are being communicated to you through this, our first gift. I am the leader of my ship and a senior member of the governing council of our planet, Zircon. My name is Zultan and my two aides are our highest priests, Zora and Beda. Our planet is in the Milky Way Galaxy, a little more than two thousand light years from your solar system. We are almost twenty-two thousand years advanced on you with our technology. We have harnessed the power of space-time travel so that we are able to traverse the galaxy almost as fast as the speed of light squared. Your Mister Einstein with his equation was a lot closer to accessing this power than he knew. But the galaxy is so vast that it has still taken much time to travel, so we relax and sleep a lot along the way. However, we have recently been blessed with a new form of space-time energy, but this is not of our doing. I will explain this to you later."

"We have come in peace as we know no violence nor aggression and we live together on our planet in total harmony with each other. It is against our nature to cause any harm to anyone, so please do not be afraid. When you wish to talk to us we will understand you. We have come here to assist you to avert a catastrophe that could destroy your beautiful world. We need to enter extensive dialogue now, so could we please be seated."

The President, still speechless, turned to his aides and motioned with his hands for them to bring the seating to the center of the room, not really knowing if the Zircons would sit or not. They did!

The President and his closest aide Ralph Lee and press secretary Lynda Lightfoot took up seating at the table opposite the three Zircons, with a number of other aides standing back several feet away. They listened intently to what the Zircon leader had to say for about fifteen minutes.

He told them a great deal – about where they had come from and other details of the Milky Way Galaxy.

Then it was Zultan himself who suggested to the President that he should go to address his people, now, as the entire world would be waiting anxiously to hear that they were in no danger from the alien visitors. He suggested that the President deliver a brief statement to the world, then return for a more comprehensive briefing on what was happening.

The President agreed.

The President and his close aides returned to the media room where everybody was waiting in total anxiety. What was the President about to say? Had they really come here in peace or were they potentially hostile? The entire history of humanity had come to the crossroads. Everything would be different from this day onwards, but for better or for worse? The expectation on the President's first address was enormous. The President faced the cameras.

"My fellow Americans, people of the world. I bring you good news. After meeting with our visitors for just this last twenty minutes, I can assure you that our visitors are here in peace. I want you all to know that I have absolutely no doubt about that, whatsoever. As you have seen, we have three visitors with us here today. Their leader introduced himself to us as the senior member of the governing council of their planet, Zircon. His name is Zultan. His two attendants are Zircon's two highest priests. Their names are Zora and Beda. Our friends can communicate with us in our own language through their technology. They want us all to know that they would never harm our planet Earth – and that they are enthralled by planet Earth's extraordinary beauty and are also enthralled by its flora and fauna, especially its people. They do, however tell me that they view Earth as being the other way up - that they see Antarctica at the top of the Earth, rather like icing on a cake and New Zealand as the top nation. I am sure the people of Invercargill will be pleased to hear that."

That initiated a lot of jubilation and cheering in New Zealand, because they had been down for so long!

"They have informed us that they are from a planet within our own Milky Way Galaxy that is more than two thousand light years away from us and that, like us, they regard the Milky Way Galaxy as home. They call their planet 'Zircon'. I believe we have a mineral here on earth by the same name. They have informed us that they were once very "primitive" (he motioned with his fingertips) like us, but that the course of their social evolution had allowed them to develop the technologies to traverse the galaxy – our galaxy – and beyond, much more quickly than we have. They have divulged that their spacecraft can travel at almost the speed of light but on a conveyor system of negative gravity that travels at the speed of light, hence they can travel almost as fast as the speed of light squared – which is something we have heard before from Mr. Einstein's equation."

"They asked us to ponder, for a moment, the rapid development of our own technology here on Earth, over the last one hundred and forty years. During that time we developed the very first motor car by Karl Benz in 1885, then the first airplane by the Wright brothers in 1903 and that within just a few decades we had motor cars and airplanes that were far advanced on these crude early models. In fact, it took just forty-six years for us to progress from the very first crude aircraft flown by the Wright brothers, to the very first passenger jet airliner – the de Havilland Comet."

"Then within just a few more decades we developed television, our computers and then advanced communication systems, such as mobile telephones, the internet and email. They asked us to ponder where our technology would take us in the next one hundred years, or one thousand years or ten thousand years or even in one million years from now. They asked us to ponder such things for a moment, then informed us that their technology is, in fact, advanced on ours by more than twenty thousand years."

"They tell me also that they know of no hostile civilizations anywhere within the Milky Way galaxy, nor within the Andromeda Galaxy, our nearest large neighbor, nor anywhere within our Local Group of more than forty galaxies. They have assured me that they are very friendly people and that they have come here to help us. Zultan explained that they have been sending droids and prototype spacecraft to this planet for several thousands of years, which explains why so many people here on Earth have witnessed UFO's and also why primitive societies have made drawings of such things over the centuries. Most of these have been unoccupied droids that were commissioned to come here for a short time and to return with information, results of experiments and technical details pertaining to space-time travel."

"Some were actually occupied spacecraft, such as those that crashed at Roswell in June 1947. I must explain that we had to keep a lid on that incident because at the time we were afraid of the consequences of revealing to the world that alien life did, in fact, exist and was able to visit our planet. We had to be mindful also of undermining long established religious beliefs that are an essential fabric of our society. I can tell you now that on this, they have assured us there is no reason to be concerned."

"This has been quite a long process for them to calculate the mathematics of traversing the Milky Way Galaxy, because of the problems they encountered with time loss. They tell us they have made some major breakthroughs recently that allow them to return to their planet at a time shortly after they left it. Most of us would be quite familiar with Einstein's assertions regarding lost time during space travel."

"They assure us that they have come here to help us."

"Zultan explained they are afraid that our world may be heading toward a nuclear catastrophe should the world allow nuclear arms to fall into the wrong hands. Zultan then explained that we do need to maintain our vigilance against terrorists to prevent a worldwide proliferation of terrorism and the subsequent acquisition of nuclear arms by terrorist groups. We have been warned that if we do not heed this advice, the governments of some nations that do possess nuclear weapons may fall into the hands of extremist factions. We have assured the Zircons that we do take this problem extremely seriously."

"However, Zultan has also stressed the need for our military will to be matched by our political will and humanitarian goodwill – for the nations of the world to take strident steps now, to engender and nurture moves to make the world a better place for everybody to live in. In particular we must be far more proactive in ameliorating our world by addressing the problems of abject poverty and starvation in poorer countries, particularly in Africa, in South America, in Afghanistan and in numerous former Soviet nations. In short, we need to cooperate a lot more to share our resources, especially our resources of food and energy."

"We have also been warned about the critical effects of global warming of our planet. They have pointed out to us that, just as we had a problem several years ago with the demise of many species of frogs in various parts of the world and the degradation of coral reefs, there are other species too - such as bees - that are now in some peril. The Zircons have warned us that if our frogs and bees die off, our trees could be next. Now ... we were asked to return to the conference room atop this building as soon as possible for further briefing ... ah ... the nature of which I am not really sure about at this point of time, but we were anxious to address the people of the world for this initial brief period to allay everybody's concerns at this most extraordinary event. I will endeavor to return to this media room to provide you all with more information, in perhaps, one hour or so. So I would ask you all to be patient during this time and please try to comfort any persons who may feel distressed."

The President ended his speech then left the media room and returned to the conference room at the top of the building with his two closest aides to spend more time with the Zircons who were still seated. They all resumed their seats. Zultan commenced his rendition of information to the President regarding the activities of extremist elements in certain countries of the world and of their plans to utilize nuclear weapons in concerted attacks against the west. Zultan stressed that much of what he would divulge would need to be treated confidentially among allied forces and not be disclosed to the public. Zultan was also quick to stress that the President needed to focus on divulging the positive aspects of his message that would engender hope for the future. He told the President of some of the wonders of the galaxy.

The President and his aides would listen intently to Zultan for the next half hour, before Zultan suggested that the President ought to once again, address the people of the world. He suggested that the President deliver a statement to the world of what he had been told, then to return for a further briefing on what was happening.

The President would agree once more.

While the President was engaged with the Zircons for the second time, CXN had taken the opportunity to seek further input from relevant professional people.

"We welcome into our Atlanta studio now the Professor of Social Sciences from Notre Dame University Professor David Jones whose specialist area of study is, in fact, the sociology of religion. Professor Jones good morning to you and thank you for giving us your time here today, we must be very fortunate that you were in Atlanta today on what really is quite an extraordinary day. Perhaps for you, in particular, as you would have a vital interest in this morning's events because of the implications, as Dr. Einstein suggested, for the world's religious beliefs, would you not?"

"Thank you, Barbara - and good morning everybody. Yes, Barbara this is something that we have never seen before and the implications for the world's religious belief systems are quite profound. There would already be a lot of people all around the world who would be regarding the appearance of a UFO like this as virtual proof that God does not exist, that Jesus Christ was not who Christian people claim him to have been and that he was merely some kind of a prophet but also, perhaps a trickster or a magician or faith healer of even some kind of a fraudster. So, an event like this has the potential to virtually turn conventional religious belief systems on their head. Of course, it still remains to be seen whether or not this UFO is a major rebuttal of religious belief systems or whether its appearance can be accommodated, somehow, by those belief systems. On my way here I chatted to a woman on the train who is a Catholic, as I am myself, who suggested that if there is intelligent life right throughout the universe, then perhaps God sent his son to all such places to be crucified or even that we humans were uniquely chosen to take the gospel to the entire universe. So that is the kind of possibility that we should keep an open mind to at this point of time, as strange as it may seem now."

"Yes, well they seem to be two very interesting perspectives that one could place on these events but Professor Jones, we have heard from a number of religious leaders here today whom we invited to call in following Dr. Einstein's advice, hoping to shed some light on just how this extraordinary event could be regarded by the world's religions and we have heard from representatives of the Jehovah's Witnesses, very briefly from The Church of Scientology, from senior ministers in the Assembly of God and very briefly also from the Bible Discernment Ministry. What seems to come through here more than anything else is that none of the people we have spoken to so far agree with the others and we can't really find a common thread here from what we have heard. So what are ordinary people supposed to think about all of this?"

"Well you've touched on the essence of the problem right there, Barbara. Most of the people you have heard from would profess one common thing, that this, their claim that they believe in the Bible. That is exactly what you will hear them say – 'we believe in the Bible'."

"Firstly on that, in some sectors of American Protestantism, such as with the Jehovah's Witnesses and the Assembly of God, this is virtually a universal catchphrase for renouncing the claimed authority of mainstream Christian churches such as the Church of England or Anglican Church, the Uniting Church, the Church of Christ and, of course, the Catholic Church in particular. It is their way of repudiating that those long-established churches have authority from Jesus Christ within their theology and invariably they see that as a way of gaining followers by coercing people to move away from traditional churches."

"Secondly, one of the main characteristics of such Protestant fundamentalism is that they do not agree with each other on many central issues and that is because they do read the Bible a lot, whereas mainstream Christian churches tend to rely upon their church hierarchy for interpretations of scripture. You see this come through quite profoundly in the teachings of the fundamentalist groups where virtually everything that they say or write they tend to endeavor to support or justify with reference to scripture. If you want to see a very good example of that you simply need to view the Bible Discernment Ministry's Statement of Faith at their own website to see that almost all of their twenty or more

'Statements of Faith', as they call them, have numerous scriptural reference. That is quite typical of the plethora of Protestant fundamentalist groups operating in the United States today and a lot of the material you will see is extremely dogmatic."

"Thirdly, when you hear somebody say that they believe in the Bible what they are really saying is that they believe in somebody else's interpretation of the Bible that has been passed on to them. Religious socialization is the powerful force at work here – people are drawn into believing a particular creed usually through their family to begin with or in later life through meeting an influential 'other'. This is something I need to return to later too if you don't mind – the question of religious identity - because it is so very significant."

"Then of course there are those who contrive their own peculiar interpretations of the Bible or an alternative document of authority and the Jehovah's Witnesses, the Mormon Church, the Bible Discernment Ministry and Scientologists are very good case studies of that too."

"Furthermore, what we invariably get from all of this is a mishmash of scriptural interpretations that really can become quite mind boggling to any reasoning person who might be genuinely seeking a close relationship with God because trying to work out who to believe would be totally confusing when so many people are denigrating so many others and each other."

"Finally, the dogmatism that comes through from Protestant fundamentalist groups really is quite vehement towards any ecumenical moves that are directed towards Christian unity and even more so toward any notions that all people who believe in God are a part of one church here on Earth - Christians, Muslims, Hindus, Buddhists etcetera. In fact, fundamentalist Protestant churches completely denounce the other main religions of the world such as Islam and Hinduism as being heretical."

"The theology of many fundamentalist groups such as Jehovah's Witnesses is essentially a litany of biblical quotes that are all carefully selected to supposedly build a picture to prove a point that has been predetermined. Quite typically learned biblical scholars will point out that the nexus between the quotes from the scripture and the point supposedly being proven is so weak as to virtually be a non-sequitur, that is, the scriptural reference could be regarded as being relevant to the point being made but not necessarily so and secondly, the same scriptural reference could be used if you were trying to prove a lot of different things."

"This is why the Jehovah's Witnesses movement is regarded as being comparatively stagnant as a religious movement in these times of extremely high evangelical outreach and recruitment of new people, especially here in the States where, for example, the Assembly of God has recruited more than twenty million followers in say, the last twenty years. The Jehovah's have a particularly dubious line of theology that seems to appeal or are typically of low intelligence and education levels and ... ah ... are more inclined than others to fall for or accept the lines of argument being put to them. Suffice to say that most people do not fall for the peculiar line of reasoning, or lack of reasoning, that is being put to them when the Jehovah's knock on your front door."

"Yes, they came to my front door once and as soon as I opened the door they popped a question that was ... ah ... 'Why can't mules breed?' Well as it so happens when I did my degree in journalism I took an elective in biology so I knew the answer to that question straight away and I started to answer them. I explained that a mule is a hybrid bred between a horse and a donkey and that as such, it has sixty-three pairs of chromosomes that don't match up, but it didn't take long for me to realize that I had already lost them in some very basic science. Then I informed them that there are some rare cases where mules have actually been known to breed."

"So I asked them why they would be asking me that question and they told me that because mules cannot breed the theory of evolution must be wrong."

"That's very interesting Tom and what you have just said reiterates the point that I am making. The people who came to your door had been given instructions to put that question to people as soon as the door opened and that people would not be able to answer the question. They had been provided with a particular line of reasoning that they, themselves, did not really know very much about, which is why your response threw them – most people wouldn't know as much about the biology of mules as you do – and then their answer to the question that supposedly denounces the theory of evolution would gain the attention of the listener to perhaps be receptive to their explanation of creationism."

"Is that what that was all about?"

"Yes they do believe that God created the world about six thousand years ago in seven solar days as accounted for in the book of Genesis. In fact, one recent study revealed that nearly forty percent of Americans do still believe in young-earth creationism."

"Well I don't!"

"Me neither!"

"Nor do I!"

"No but you three are journalists, you have been educated at the college level and have a better understanding of the world and science than most Americans do. You would find that belief in young-earth creationism diminishes as you go higher up the education level line where more people believe in old-earth creationism – they believe God did create the universe but at the time of the big bang – as I do myself."

"So people with a college education are less inclined to believe in the Genesis account of creation and are more inclined to believe in the theory of evolution, than are people without a college education?"

"Yes, Barbara, of people with a college education probably only about twenty percent still believe in the Genesis version of creation, whereas, among people who did not complete high school, probably fifty percent do. But belief in the theory of evolution does not negate one's belief in God. Young-earth creationists might have you believe that but educated people are far more inclined, than others, to believe that the account of creation in Genesis is metaphorical and that God created the universe so that life on Earth could evolve the way that it has. I am a Catholic and we don't see any contradiction at all between believing in God and accepting the theory of evolution."

"So how do the young-earth creationists explain dinosaur fossils if they believe that God created the world about six thousand years ago?"

"Not just dinosaur fossils Alex but consider, too, sedimentary rock formations that can take hundreds of millions of years to develop. The answer is they can explain that away. When dinosaur fossils were first discovered in England and here in the States in the early nineteenth century, the creationists explained that God had made the dinosaur fossils for the scientists. They said the same of sedimentary rock when geologists started to point out the massive time frames involved in its production beneath the sea."

"Of course, the Jehovah's Witnesses are not alone in that belief and to the contrary, the Assembly of God is experiencing an enormous expansionism despite its fundamentalist teachings. But Assembly of God teachings are not as banal as those of the Jehovah's Witnesses and they are certainly upbeat in the way they are presented and, indeed, marketed."

"Why do people carry on that way, as you said Professor, espousing their own views to the point of denigrating others so intensely?"

"There are several reasons for that Barbara and the sociology of religion as a discipline is always developing its hypotheses and theories about this and certainly the 'us and them' syndrome of sociology comes into this quite strongly here. We feel more secure with the 'us' - that is ourselves - if we can identify the 'them' in our society - that being the others or the opposition - because that tends to strengthen the bonds between us. You see this most profoundly in sport for example, where we stick together closely with people who cheer for our team and we can literally feel quite malicious toward or even hate the opposition. This loathing of the others can also contribute to our self-identity and belonging to our own group."

"Well we see that every day in sport somewhere, don't we, perhaps in ice hockey more than anywhere else – it's not exactly a 'do unto others' sport now is it?"

"No and apart from that there is quite some American ego involved here – we are the biggest and the best and some feel they need to act like it. So you often see a fringe group develop and a driving force behind them is the putting forward of one's self as being privy to enlightenment and we need to tell others, so it's a case of 'I am going to tell everybody what I think and you all better listen up now'. This often involves being predisposed to criticizing others as a means of legitimizing one's self."

"And in more recent times we have witnessed the proliferation of what you might call 'dollar driven theology', such as prosperity doctrine and all that comes with it. There are a lot of people out there now who have become full time ministers of religion and they derive their very substantial incomes from this because they virtually demand that followers provide quite extensive financial support they refer to as tithings. Now in order to start up a new church or an offspring of an existing church people sometimes have to justify their own existence by being critical of others. We see that come through a lot now, actually, especially on the internet where social forum and chat groups are meeting and breeding grounds for putting one's own theology forward and renouncing others. The modern-day technology gives everybody a chance to have their say, somewhere."

"Of course, one of the reasons you do hear so many Protestants say they believe in the Bible, is that it is their way of repudiating the authority of the Catholic Church and its doctrine of papal infallibility. So very often you hear Protestant preachers saying 'we believe in the Bible' as the ultimate authority of God' and this is essentially their way of repudiating the authority claimed by the Catholic Church."

"The Catholic Church on the other hand points out that according to the scriptures Jesus gave all authority in heaven and on earth to Saint Peter whom he instated as the very first head of the Church of Rome, when he said 'whatever you bind on earth shall be bound in heaven and whatever you loosen on earth shall be loosened in heaven'."

"The problem the Catholic Church does have is that the history of the papacy is littered with instances that would make any reasoning person doubt the concept of papal infallibility and I speak as a Catholic myself. Perhaps in recent times the stance of the Vatican during World War II in failing to denounce that Nazi's is a case in point and, more recently, on questions pertaining to sexuality such as de-facto relationships and bi-sexuality. The Catholic Church flies in the face of economic reality that precludes many people from marriage and modern medicine which has already gone quite some way to explaining that many genuinely bi-sexual people are born with chromosomes of both the male and female gender and we see that very clearly in intersex individuals, where an intersex individual may have biological characteristics of both the male and the female sexes."

"But for all the problems it causes between Catholics and Protestants in ecumenism and the prospect of a long-term reconciliation or unification, the Catholic Church would be well advised to attenuate the concept of Papal Infallibility somehow, or to dispense with the idea completely."

"So Barbara the reasons for that level of religious discord are many and varied and I certainly hope that perhaps later today we can discuss this even further."

"Thank you Professor David Jones - you have raised some very interesting discussion points there that we should come back to later. Right now we have a representative online from the Church of England direct from London in the most Reverend Bishop Nigel Clancy, the Archbishop of Canterbury. Good morning to you Reverend Clancy."

"Good afternoon, or should I say good morning to all in America it is, of course mid-afternoon here in London, I thank you for allowing me to discuss this situation with you here today."

"Yes we would be very interested to hear from you since you are a representative of an established conservative Christian Church. We have heard this morning from a number of religious leaders here in the United States and from Professor David Jones from the University of Notre Dame who is with us now. Reverend Clancy as a senior bishop in the Church of England can you please tell us, what is your initial response to these very peculiar events here today in New York?"

"I suppose the first thing that I want to say to everybody is that we ought not to worry too much about this event. It is important that we heed the plea from the President of the

United States, who as I understand it, is meeting with the three visitors from the spacecraft as we speak and I believe he hopes to address the nation again very soon, and remain calm. It is very encouraging that the initial message that has come forth is they are here in peace and now we have some idea of where they have come from and, of course, we now know with great certainty that there is intelligent life elsewhere in the universe, which I must say I find rather encouraging."

"Ah ... not sure that people would have been expecting you to put forth that viewpoint your Grace, I suppose most people would be thinking that the appearance of aliens here on earth could cause some major disruption to the classical teachings of all Christian Churches and, indeed, of all religions actually."

"Well that may be the expected view Barbara, but here in the church we tend to be very circumspect about jumping to conclusions whenever anything strange or unusual happens, such as the discovery of the crystal skulls for example and we tread very carefully with prudence. We will have a much better idea of what we are dealing with here when the President has been fully briefed - and we have a chance to carefully consider all of the implications for our religions."

"With respect your Grace, an alien spaceship has just landed here on earth and you seem to be advocating a sit back, wait and see approach when perhaps all of your people are probably feeling rather perplexed if not totally bewildered by all of this already. Don't you think that they deserve to hear how the church might reconcile this event with its traditional, historical teachings that we are unique in the universe and created by God to be reunited with Him?"

"Well at this point of time Alex we do not know a lot about them and we must keep an open mind, they might be very spiritual people themselves we will just have to wait and see. I can't help thinking right now about the Letter of Saint Paul to the Romans where Saint Paul states that God has given all of us the power to perceive Him, His eternal power and His divine glory, in the things that He has made. I would contend already that it is distinctly possible that God has created life right throughout the universe and that all intelligent beings have been blessed with the very same ability to perceive Him. I certainly hope that to be the case and I would not be at all surprised if our visitors are very spiritual people themselves."

"Hey, you have got to be kidding me, I'm sorry your Grace I am just having a little bit of trouble with that idea already. You are saying that these aliens might be religious or spiritual people too, like us. Ah … how could that come about, do you think that Jesus might have gone to their planet too?"

"Look, Alex, I don't regard your response with any surprise on my part, I am sure that a lot of people would feel the same way that you do, but consider that if you do believe in what Saint Paul wrote in his letter to the Romans then any intelligent life form could conceivably perceive God in nature in the very same way that we do. It is a basic tenet of anthropology that primitive societies here on earth perceived God in the wonders of nature. In fact, every society has perceived God, especially in nature and I suppose that our perception of God developed as we did, from being a primitive man to being Homo sapiens as we are now. What I am saying is that we reached a point of development as homo-sapiens up to two hundred thousand years ago and we became aware of a deity perhaps sometime prior to Cro-Magnon man. In fact, some evidence points toward both Neanderthal man and Cro-Magnon man being involved in religious-type ceremony and certainly tribal life in all societies since at least ten thousand years ago is characterized by religious ceremony."

"I would hasten to add that our perception of God in nature can perhaps, best be seen in our beautiful flora and fauna. You just have to marvel at the wonderment of flowers or butterflies, for example, to be quite blown away with the feeling that there is an almighty powerful force at work here in creation. A lot of people would experience that watching David Attenborough's programs."

"He's an atheist!"

"Yes Alex, he is an atheist by choice - and I believe I have heard his exposition on the reasons why. It seems that for all the marvels that he is aware of in nature he has some difficulty accepting that a God could preside over so much chaos and catastrophe in nature also. Well that is his choice and he seems to base his decision on an assumption that death is something that is undesirable but Christians regard death as the gateway to life so I don't really see where David Attenborough is coming from on that one."

"I would also hasten to add that since our visitors have seemingly come here in peace and that, too, points to the level of sophistication of their civilization and perhaps even to their possible spirituality."

"But where would this put Jesus?"

"We have to maintain our faith in God. Questions about the implications of this for the account of Jesus on earth, claiming as He did, that he was the son of God and questions of His rising from the dead will need to be considered in due course. I would like to wait until I hear more from the visitors before speculating about whether our historical account of the life of Jesus Christ has been discredited somehow. For now my advice to Christians everywhere and to all religious people of all persuasions – be they Muslim or Hindu or Jew or Buddhist - would simply be, to maintain your faith in God."

"Okay we might have to leave that there for now your Grace, we certainly appreciate your input here today, I am sure that a lot of believers will find some comfort in those words. Perhaps we can return to the bishop a little later also."

"Thank you Barbara Foster!"

"Professor Jones, what would you have to say about that?"

"Oh, I think he hit the nail on the head right from the outset, actually ..."

"You gotta be kidding me!"

"Alex! Bishop Clancy has advocated circumspection and due prudence in a situation like this and there is a lot of wisdom in what he says. No doubt you have heard it said that the wheels of bureaucracy turn slowly, well there are probably few bureaucracies where the wheels turn more slowly that in a conservative religious institution. The Church of England is not about to pre-empt any conclusions that may be drawn when we do obtain more information about where these alien visitors are from. As he said they may well be very spiritual beings who have religious ceremony of their own and, if so, we could all be worshipping the same God."

"Professor Jones we did hear Bishop Clancy refer there to the world's other main religions too - Islam, Hinduism, Judaism and Buddhism - and that might seemingly put him at odds with our American Protestants that we heard from earlier ... ah ... both the Jehovah's Witnesses and the Assembly of God in particular, who have put forth the view that only Christians are going to be saved - well actually, the Jehovah's put the view that only they will be saved - should this be the second coming of Jesus Christ. Our Assembly of God spokespeople put the view that only Christians who are born again and pray in tongues and become tithers will be saved. Professor Jones what do you make of all of this?"

"Bishop Clancy is espousing the modern-day view of the mainstream Christian churches Tom – the Church of England but also of the Catholic Church ..."

"Why haven't we heard from the Catholic Church yet?"

"Well Alex, you might find the Catholic Church is still preparing its initial response that may be even more circumspect than that of Bishop Clancy. But coming back to where I was, you will find an enormous chasm in the doctrine of the mainstream churches and the American fundamentalist Protestant churches towards the world's other main religions. Of course we do have some American Protestant churches that are in the mainstream too, such as the Baptist Church, the Methodist Church, the Congregational Church and the Church of Christ, but the fundamentalist churches are so very dogmatic and take scriptural verse so literally, providing that serves a predetermined purpose, that it seems it will take a long time for world ecumenism to bridge that chasm. The fundamentalist churches like things just the way they are, after all, religion is big business here in America."

"So are we able to digress here for a minute so that you can tell us more about the disposition of the mainstream churches toward Islam and Hinduism etc."

"Well Tom, historically, perhaps up to the late 1950's the Catholic Church and the Church of England were rather similar on such issues as the fundamentalists are today but a lot of things changed enormously within the Catholic Church with the advent of the Second Vatican Council. The election of Pope John XXIII changed everything. Up to that point of time a lot of teaching in Catholic schools for example would have been almost as dogmatic as most of the fundamentalist Protestant churches are today. Some Catholic clergy, too, were preaching that only Christians would be granted a place in heaven, Protestants were regarded by some Catholic clergy as lesser Christians who, at best, would spend a long time in Purgatory before being admitted into heaven, other religions may have been regarded as heathen who would never go to heaven but a lot of the changes in Catholic thinking within the Vatican were simply not passed on to Catholic people at all. But the changes were taking place and the election of John XXIII was a symptom rather than a cause of the changes."

"Within just a few years we saw the inception of Mass being said in people's native language – in America in English rather than in Latin. Some of the silly doctrine was dispensed with. I have a friend who tells me that one Friday he agonized for hours before eating a piece of hamburger from fear of being damned to hell for eating meat on a Friday. He then rushed off to confession. Up until Vatican II eating meat on a Friday was regarded as a mortal sin worthy of eternal damnation."

"Why?"

"Because Jesus was crucified on a Friday. That was a part of the ritualism that the Catholic Church had in place at the time, that out of deference to our Lord we abstained from eating meat on Friday's. It was very good for all fish and chip shop owners because they had a lot of Catholic customers every Friday but the validity of it and certain other things was called into question by Vatican II."

"Thank God for that!"

"Probably!"

"What other things?"

"Oh, compulsory attendance at Mass on holy days of the year, what they referred to as holy days of obligation ... ah ... All Saints Day, Ascension Thursday and so on. But the big changes were in the disposition of the Catholic Church, at the top, towards Protestants and Muslims and Jews and so on as well as to theological questions pertaining to Purgatory and Limbo and the reasons behind that doctrine."

"Ah ... can you run those terms passed me again, I don't think I have heard of those before now."

"Well, Alex, you might just have to look into those via Wikipedia in more detail but, essentially, Purgatory and Limbo represented the Catholic Church's way of dealing with some theological paradox, such as the eternal destiny of people who were rather like half-baked Christians - if I could convey the meaning that way - and of indigenous people who lived before Christ or of the unbaptized still born child."

"So today you would find that the Catholic Church is far removed from that line of religious theology and does, in fact, believe that God embraces all people who believe in him and choose to worship any way they wish and, for that matter, possibly even others too who are not overtly religious or spiritual people."

"So are you saying that the Catholic Church now believes that Muslim people and Hindu people will go to Heaven, is that what you are saying?"

"That is exactly what I am saying! It is not the formal adherence to a religious movement that is critical but the way a person lives their life. I think you will find that the modern-day Catholic priest would subscribe to that theology."

"What – with the blessing of the church hierarchy in Rome?"

"Oh yes, without a doubt - that level of understanding of the world's religions emanates from Rome. So it has, in fact, come from the top, from the papacy. In fact some very eminent Catholic theologians have espoused that very view since the time of Vatican II in a concept it refers to as the 'anonymous Christian', meaning that a person can be Christian or Christ-like in the way they live lives of goodness without being overtly religious. Hence, all good people go to heaven because Jesus died for our sins. This theology is not entirely without its detractors and as much as some people might object to being referred to as Christians, hey, if you are a good person and you love your neighbor as yourself and you 'do unto others' etcetera then you are, in fact, Christ like. So what does it matter if somebody refers to you as an anonymous Christian – Jesus Christ was and is the epitome of all goodness."

"Well Professor Jones we might have to consult our Catholic representative when ... if they call in, about some of these things."

"Barbara I am wondering why we had to wait for aliens to come here before we had this discussion!"

"Yes that's a good point Alex."

"Now we are receiving word, are we, that something is happening again at the United Nations building. It seems the President may be on his way out of the conference room returning to the media room already with some more information for us. So very shortly we will cross live again to our media correspondent team in the UN building."

Chapter 7

By now Michael and Chrissy had made their way home – Michael to be with his family and Chrissy to her husband Graham. Michael opened his front door to be greeted by his two young daughters.

"Daddy, daddy, we saw you on television and you were kissing a lady."

Michael was stunned! His first thought was that his wife was somewhere in the house and she was obviously aware of what had been screened on television. He would have to face her and would have to explain. Was this going to be the end of his marriage? He felt totally numb and very nervous. His heart was racing. He knew his wife Julie would be totally shocked, disappointed in him and extremely upset.

"Okay girls the lady was very upset, okay and daddy was trying to help her, now ... ah ... please go and play somewhere because daddy has to talk to mommy okay."

The girls ran off and Michael walked through the living room, into the family room and through the kitchen. He then saw his wife sitting on the settee in the sunroom, where she was facing the outside garden with her back turned to him as he walked into the sunroom. Michael looked at her as he took up a seat in front of her and slightly left, but Julie simply stared straight ahead at the outside garden. He really didn't know what to say so he tried to gather his thoughts as if to find some acceptable explanation.

Julie simply sat there staring straight ahead as a minute or two passed, then she took a deep breath as if to signal to Michael that he needed to say something.

"I suppose you saw me on television giving that woman a kiss!"

Julie blinked then her eyes rolled left to stare at him, a sullen look on her face.

"How long has this been going on?"

"One day! Just one day!"

"You mean, last night? When you worked back?"

He nodded his head ashamedly and solemnly.

"It just happened. We were there alone, there had never been any inkling of any feelings between us, ever, in fact ... ah ... never a single word had ever passed between us on a personal level and ... ah ... we have been in that same situation before, where we had to work alone together after hours. There had been some jocularity but never anything personal."

"Until last night - so what changed that made last night so different? Michael!"

"We were ... ah ... talking about people we worked with and how Bob and Dave had found new partners after their marriage breakup. Then she raised the matter of her husband Graham and how he was so cold and aloof most of the time and that she did not enjoy a good relationship with him – that she suspected he might have a lover where he works at the bank."

"Then she asked me about us."

Julie looked at Michael intently.

"And what did you say about us, Michael?"

"I said, yeah, things are okay, I love my wife and I have two very beautiful daughters that she has given me and ... ah ... I am content with my marriage to Julie ..."

"But then she said 'just content' did she?"

"Well, yes she did."

"And how did you respond to that, Michael, my husband?"

Michael took a deep breath as if to prepare himself for what he needed to express about his innermost feelings about his marriage, to his wife Julie."

"I ... ah ... told her that things could be better."

Julie took a deep breath then let out a long sigh before putting the obvious question.

"I suppose that means you think you should have a better sex life Michael. Which is why you fell into the trap of this woman who has a husband who is cold and aloof and is probably having an affair?"

Michael took a deep breath then looked down and covered his face with his hands. For him the moment of truth had arrived that he would need to disclose to his wife that she did not meet his needs.

"Look I know just from talking to people I work with or men from the golf club that some couples do enjoy a far better sex life that we do, Julie. Some men have told me that their wife makes love with them three times a week, religiously. One golfer told me that when he has sex with his wife, she wants to have sex for a couple of hours before she goes to sleep. With us, now, it is only when you either feel inclined, which is not very often, or you feel sorry for me or you detect that perhaps I need some loving. Let's face it, we probably enjoy intimacy, on average, about twice per month now."

"And you need more loving than I give to you."

Michael did not want to answer in the affirmative on that one, even though that was his answer within his own mind, for he knew that would be the wrong thing to say to a woman.

"I would indulge in a more ... ah ... expressive sex life if the opportunity was there, with you, I mean."

"So this Christine, then she said something to you, no doubt, that was essentially a proposition – is that right?"

"She said 'well there's nothing you can do about that, is there'."

"And you said?"

"No! I'll just have to grin and bear it."

"Then she said?"

"She said ... 'well perhaps I can help you a little'."

Which you would have taken as an open invitation to have an affair with her, in the office, last night. Right?"

"I told her that I love my wife, Julie. I said I am married and I was raised as a Christian and to have an affair would be sinful. I told her I don't believe in extra-marital relationships."

"So how did that develop from there?"

"She came over to me and put her hands on my shoulders and said 'I am sure the good Lord will understand – you do a lot for your family'. But then she kissed me."

"Passionately?"

Michael nodded his head.

"I felt something I had not felt for a long time, Julie, not since we were dating many years ago. It was … irresistible. As you know she is a very attractive woman. Before I knew it, she had her hand on … my body. She knew what she was doing – before I could say anything more, she had dropped her underwear onto the floor. I just couldn't control myself just thinking of how easy it would be and how good it would feel … to go inside her. She thrust her body against mine then she proceeded to undo my trousers. Even then I was trying to resist her but when she went down and took me in her mouth there was nothing I could do to prevent the inevitable. Then she pulled me down onto the floor and I lay on top of her. From the time she kissed me to when we lay on the floor, it was all over in just a couple of minutes."

Julie just sat there thinking and shaking her head. Her husband had fallen for an age-old trick that she had read about in a women's magazine. The formula was well prescribed and seemed to work every time, according to women who had seduced men – "start with a passionate kiss then go for their cock, with your mouth", as one woman had put it "they will have to make a snap decision and they will be putty in your hands. It's the power of the pussy and most men can't say no".

"I ... ah ... have no intention of going anywhere with Chrissy again, Julie. What happened last night is it – all over. I will never do anything like that ever again".

He was already thinking about the implications of losing his family – his beautiful wife and his two beautiful daughters, which was now a reality to him, for he did not know what his wife was thinking, what she would do. But deep within his mind he knew that earlier that morning he was actually very excited about his new-found love and looking forward so much to many intimate moments with the woman who had rekindled his love life. Now he was in a position where reality had struck home - and he would have to re-assess.

"You do realize that this changes everything, don't you Michael?"

As she looked at him the tears started rolling down her face.

"You realize that I will never be able to trust you again the way that I have up until now. I thought I was married to a good Christian man, a man who plays golf on Saturdays, yes, but then he goes to church with me on Sundays. Didn't you give any thought to the Lord when she kissed you?"

"Ah ... I guess I just got caught up in the moment. No I didn't think of the Lord when she kissed me, it all happened so quickly and I got caught up in the feelings."

"You are supposed to be a good Christian man, Michael – a man who can say no to temptation from the devil, Michael. He got the better of you, didn't he, just as Pastor James said he can."

"I guess I now know what Pastor James meant. I am sorry, Julie, I truly am. I know I will have to do my best now to be the man you thought of me as."

"I think it will be best if I take the girls and move over to mom and dad's place for now. I am going to have to give this some thought."

"And I guess you want me to stay here?"

"That goes without saying. I will need to have a long talk to Pastor James about this, Michael."

"You don't need to go Julie. We can go talk to Pastor James together – try to work through this, you know. I feel terrible for what I have done and ... ah ... I know I can change and become a better husband for you and a better father for the girls. I just need another chance."

"I'm not exactly in a frame of mind for giving second chances flippantly Michael. I will take the girls to mom's today and give it all some serious thought. You stay here."

Julie arose and left the room, going straight to her bedroom to pack some clothes. Michael's phone rang – it was Bob.

"Michael I thought I had better touch base with you to see if everything is okay ... ah ... you left today with Chrissy and my Narelle saw you on television so where are you now?"

"I am at home with Julie, Bob. Julie saw us too and she is already planning to move out of here today and go to her parents' place for a while with the girls."

"Good Lord, Michael, hey if you need someone to talk to you feel free to come right over here, okay and you can stay here the night."

"Yeah thanks Bob I might take you up on that offer. I don't cherish the thought of being alone here tonight."

"Well we will see you later, just come over whenever, okay."

"Okay, thanks Bob."

Julie took her suitcase into the girls' room and proceeded to start packing a suitcase for each of them.

Michael stood at the door watching her.

"Julie I will be going to stay at Bob's for the night. Can you ... ah ... let me know how soon we can go see Pastor James and ... ah ... I will see if I can tee up a liaison for us with Father Dougal."

"I will see if Pastor James can talk to us tomorrow, Michael. Just leave me be for now, please. In fact, it might be better for you if you leave for Bob's before I leave."

Despite what he had done, Julie did not want to leave the house with the girls with Michael there watching them go. She felt that would be very difficult for him. She was hurting but she was trying to remain calm and collected in the circumstances.

Michael went to their room and packed his suitcase, including his golf attire, for tomorrow was Saturday, his day out with the boys. He walked past the girls' room where Julie was still packing and said his goodbye.

"Julie, please find it within your heart to forgive me. I let my guard down for just a moment and it is something I will never do again. I love you Julie. I really do love you."

"We will talk tomorrow with Pastor James."

"And possibly Father Dougal!"

"Yes, possibly Father Dougal too."

Michael was wary of going to see Pastor James only, without also talking to Father Dougal because he was aware of Pastor James being ultra conservative and would probably counsel Julie in private that her husband had been taken by Satan and there was no hope. He had heard Pastor James on many occasions lecture on the power of Satan. He knew that his Catholic priest would be far more conciliatory and would hear his confession, in the Sacrament of Penance, in which God would forgive him of his wrongdoing.

Michael left for Bob's house and Julie was close behind him.

Once he was on the road, Michael decided to call Bob's house to let them know that he was on his way. Bob's wife Rachael answered the telephone.

"Hello Rachael, its Michael, just calling to let you and Bob know that I will be there within half an hour."

"Oh Michael, Bob has gone out in a huge hurry, he got a call from Christine and she seemed really distressed, so he dropped everything and went."

"Christine! Okay thank you Rachael I will call Bob on his mobile."

Michael dialed Bob's number.

"Bob Rachael told me you had to duck over to Chrissy's place in a hurry. Is everything okay?"

There were a few seconds of silence.

"Jesus, Michael! No, I'm afraid not. The police are here. Michael, there has been a shooting here, at Chrissy's house. The police have been told by some witnesses here that they heard two shots. I cannot confirm this yet but it seems that two people, a man and a woman, are dead inside this house in what looks to be a case of murder suicide. Michael – I'm afraid we might have lost Chrissy."

Chapter 8

Back in the studio CXN was ready to cross once again to the Presidential address.

The President and his aides returned to the media room where everybody was waiting anxiously once more. The President seemed to be smiling. What would the President say this time?

"My fellow Americans, people of the world. As you know I have now been in dialogue with our friends from the planet Zircon for almost one hour since my previous brief to you and I have to tell you that I am absolutely astonished at what I have been informed of here this morning."

"The Zircon people have informed us that they do possess detailed knowledge of our galaxy, the Milky Way, for they have traversed the entire galaxy with technology that is presently beyond our comprehension. They confirm that there are more than three hundred billion stars in our Milky Way Galaxy. Of these, more than sixty billion stars have planets that orbit the parent star. They are able to readily identify stars that are in the second stage of their life, similar to our own sun. They are able to identify such stars from a great distance and they confirm that of these sixty billion solar systems, there are more than seventeen million planets that support life within our own galaxy. Of these, there are hundreds of planets that are conducive to supporting plant and animal life, as we know it."

"They have informed us that these planets have an atmosphere very similar to the atmosphere here on earth, that these planets have oceans of water, the oceans have currents and they give rise to rainfall. These planets also have dry land in the forms of both continents and islands, with both flora and fauna in advanced stages of evolution."

"Their home planet is smaller than Earth but much brighter as it orbits a parent star that is much brighter than our sun. This is why they have evolved to be smaller than we are and why they have such large very dark eyes. This way they don't need to wear sunglasses."

Everybody chuckled.

"They tell us that within our galaxy there are some very large habitable planets, several times the size of Earth. There are also some habitable planets that are smaller than Earth, rather like the size of Mars but even smaller."

"They have told me of one larger planet that has a mountain that is larger than Olympus Mons on Mars - about seventy thousand feet high with a vertical cliff over thirty thousand feet high. That vertical cliff face is higher than Mt Everest is above sea level.

That planet has a river about twice the size of the Amazon and with a waterfall that is four miles wide and over two thousand feet high. The planet has trees over eight hundred feet high and has reptiles like Tyrannosaurus Rex that are nearly two hundred feet tall, as well as many dinosaurs with six legs. It also has some nasty spiders like Australia's funnel web spider, but the size of our domestic cats and that run extremely fast. There are all kinds of fauna and flora that we can't possibly imagine – such as a carnivorous plant that is similar to our Venus Fly Trap but is about the size of a bus and eats animals the size of our largest cats – and I mean lions. Another carnivorous plant hangs from trees or overhanging cliffs and builds a web the same way that spiders do here on Earth - and they catch their prey by trapping animals in their web and then hauling them upwards."

"This planet also generates ocean waves more than three hundred feet high – essentially, everything about this planet is gargantuan. Its oceans support sharks that are fifty yards long and whales that are more than two hundred yards long. Some fish have wings that allow them to fly for miles without returning to the water. Imagine glorious multi-colored butterflies the size of eagles."

"They have told us of one smaller planet has mice the size of ants, has cats the size of our mice, has elephants the size of our dogs and miniature forests the size of our maze plantations."

"Some planets are brighter than Earth and some not so bright. One solar system has three planets approximately the size of Earth that lay within the habitable zone. They know of at least six planets that are virtually identical to Earth except that they are not tilted like our planet is, except one, which is tilted twenty degrees and has seasons very similar to ours here on earth. They tell me that this particular planet is virtually identical to our own planet Earth. It has tectonic plates and continents, it has oceans with islands and seasons too, it has advanced forms of animal life including mammals and reptiles, but many times more edible vegetables and fruits than we have here on earth."

"I must admit that in listening to our friends explain such things I was completely transfixed, as I expect you too, are transfixed in trying to imagine such things. It seems that our galaxy and the planets within it are so much more wondrous that we could possibly imagine. Which augers well for, perhaps, a very exciting future for us. I must hasten to add that at this point of time the Zircon people have not yet indicated that they have come here to assist us to achieve this. But let's keep our fingers and toes crossed."

"Our friends have also divulged that there are even more habitable planets in the Andromeda Galaxy, which is considerably older and larger than our Milky Way Galaxy and, as such, has a far greater proportion of second stage suns and their respective solar systems. I should add here that for a star to have planets that contain the elements that planets in our solar system have, the star needs to be in its second life. The elements come about when a first-life star implodes upon itself and this implosion causes a nuclear reaction that actually gives rise to the abundance of elements ... ah ... carbon, magnesium, sulfur, silver, gold, uranium, as we know them."

"Now on the question of how they got here or ... how do they traverse the galaxy? They tell us that gravitational waves travel at the speed of light squared and that their propulsion system utilizes gravitational waves that are captured by an electromagnetic plasma coil. They are able to travel almost as fast as the speed of light squared because, apparently, these gravitational waves travel in every conceivable direction simultaneously – as if they are a type of omnipresent conveyor system. Their technology, therefore, allows them to warp light and space-time. With the Milky Way being approximately one hundred thousand light years across, they are able to traverse the galaxy from one side to the other in approximately eight of our months. At this speed it took them almost eighteen years to reach the Andromeda Galaxy, which they have been researching now for almost six hundred earth years."

"Now they are on the brink of discovering ways of travelling between galaxies utilizing what we have come to term 'wormholes', which should allow them to explore the universe much more quickly. They have also begun experiments aimed at traversing the far reaches of the universe by utilizing the black holes at the center of galaxies, for they have reason to believe that these are doorways to either distant parts of the universe, or even to parallel universes."

"They have calculated that there are more than four hundred billion galaxies in the universe known to them and that many galaxies are many times larger than our Milky Way. The largest galaxy they know of is more than six million light years in diameter – but I didn't tell them that we knew that too. I suppose to anyone who has pondered the extraordinary images of the Hubble Deep Space Field at our NASA website, this estimate would not surprise. They have also informed us that some galaxies have evolved in such a way that they are far more conducive to the creation of habitable planets than our own Milky Way Galaxy or the Andromeda Galaxy. From their observations, it seems that some galaxies have literally thousands of planets that could be habitable by us humans."

"They will explain more to me on this during their third and final information session. I have been asked to attend this third and final briefing with the Zircons and to then return to you again after they leave our planet here today."

"Oh, by the way, in case you are wondering and many of you probably are, our friends do possess some protective weapons very similar to the 'phasers' like those we are familiar with from Star Trek, but they will never use these with hostility against another civilized race. Though they ... ah ... have used them occasionally to stun some giant funnel web spiders."

Once again everybody chuckled.

The President then left the media room and returned to the roof top conference room.

"Wow, that is just so amazing, what they have divulged to us through our President in the very short time that they have been here among us – that there are so many planets out there in our own Milky Way Galaxy that are going to be inhabitable by us ...ah... if we can ever get to those planets, wow I am ... ah ... just completely dumbstruck by this. What do you boys think?"

"Hey I too am just blown away by this ... ah ... words are hard to find to express what I am feeling right now. It is as if the entire world or even our entire existence as a race, as the human race, has just been completely turned upside down just in these last couple of hours ... you know ... we are never going to be the same again. Alex what do you think?"

"Well I am almost speechless Tom, but, hey I'm with you guys on this although ... ah ... I have been rather expecting that someday something like this could happen, you know, I keep up to speed a little on the discipline of metaphysics and ... ah ... Dr. Einstein is one of my favorite people and I have heard him talk of the possibilities that someday there could be another civilization present itself to us here on earth, but, geez, now that it is actually happening, I've got to say that even I feel quite numb, you know. What do you think Professor Jones?"

"Unbelievable! Just absolutely unbelievable. But I must say I am already looking forward immensely to undertaking some sociological analyses of their society when I get my chance to go to Zircon."

"Hahaha! If you get your chance, but gee, isn't it exciting to know that there are so many different types of worlds out there in our own galaxy that the President has disclosed here this morning, his having been briefed on this by the visitors – well he called them our friends didn't he and that … that is so re-assuring to hear him say that and I am sure that people all over the world will be very relieved right now to know that these alien, well perhaps we shouldn't be calling them alien any more, hey, they are well, almost like us in so many ways. But guys we have so many things to discuss here now I am not sure where to start – we have the appearance of the aliens themselves which is just so much like people have been testifying to for decades but also the details the President mentioned about so many planets and planets where life is both so much larger and so much smaller than life here on earth."

"That's right Barbara, where do we go next I think perhaps for the sake of keeping this positive let's talk about those planets, some so much larger than planet Earth with giant forests and huge dinosaurs, some with six legs, my God what are they something like a reptilian insect and spiders the size of cats and on the smaller planets mice the size of ants, geeze, where do we go on this? Perhaps it could be the moment to call upon some top-level biologists and I wonder what the man himself, David Attenborough…"

"Sir David!"

"Oh yes I do apologize, Sir David Attenborough, I certainly would like to pick his brains right at the moment. Perhaps we can raise him to come on-line to talk to us, now that would be so very special."

"I think we have someone working on contacting Sir David now."

"And what about that waterfall – four miles wide and over two thousand feet high, hey I gotta see that I tell ya."

"But you could become a meal for a giant T-Rex if you go there Alex."

"Or a funnel web spider!"

"Yes, or a funnel web spider, now that would be really scary."

"Well it certainly places a different perspective on our own planet Earth doesn't it because, our planet is just a particular combination of physical circumstances that can vary so much depending on so many things like, proximity to a parent star, the abundance of water, gravity, the evolution of life, it really seems now to be a mishmash of so many factors. Perhaps we have tended to believe that, because life here on earth is the way it is that life everywhere else must be fairly similar, but hey, trees that are more than eight hundred feet high, my God!"

"Now for those of you who might just be tuning in or have perhaps missed what the President has just a short time ago had to say in his address to the people, well, to the whole world actually, our visitors have today provided the President with details of other worlds – of other planets within our own Milky Way Galaxy that are inhabited by a very peculiar range of life and also of very extraordinary geological or geographical features and that these exoplanets, as we have come to call them, are so totally abundant in our galaxy as to be pervasive, or numerous. Also that there are planets out there that are so much larger than our own planet Earth and many that are very much smaller and that thousands of these planets, both larger and smaller do in fact support life as we know it. In fact our visitors have told the President that there are planets in our galaxy that have dinosaurs and huge insects and a much wider range of life forms than we presently have here on earth. So this really is becoming more extraordinary as the day progresses.

"Excuse me Barbara, I think we should also point out to all viewers that the aliens, or should I say our visitors, do profess to be high priests from their home planet and that seems to imply that they are also very spiritual people. I thought we should mention that for the sake of all of your viewers who believe fervently in God and perhaps for now let's keep an open mind as to whether they believe in a God who created the universe or perhaps a God who initiated the big bang or whatever, let's just wait and see what they have to say about this question of religion and deity. I was particularly interested that they have said we have nothing to be concerned about with respect of our religious beliefs and I am wondering what they mean by that."

"Yes that's certainly an imperative to mention that right at this point of time Professor Jones, thank you. That puts the advice from Bishop Clancy in a more positive light now doesn't it Alex?"

"Yeah I guess so but I am still yet to be convinced that this event here today does not cast a huge question mark over religion per se and over the life and death of Jesus Christ in particular."

"Okay more on that after the President's third and final briefing from the Zircons. Now perhaps we should speculate about their journey to come here to our planet Earth today. We now know just a little about their transportation system and how they traverse such enormous distances considering that their planet is some two thousand light years from planet Earth. That really is quite mind-blowing to think they have the technology to be capable of doing that. The President did state that they travel faster than the speed of light squared which sounds like part of the Einstein equation $E=MC$ squared and I guess that would take a whole lot of time off getting anywhere."

"Yes that is so interesting because even now we do have our own meta-physicists working on that type of theoretical modelling of devising a craft that distorts light so that it warps and allows a traveler to virtually take a short cut through space and I have also seen a presentation by Dr. Hal Puthoff who talks about a spaceship traveling near light speed but also being on a type of conveyor that itself is moving near light speed so that could be the general idea there that our visitors have been able to harness."

"That's very interesting Alex! Now we have a representative from the Council on American-Islamic Relations Mr. Ibrahim Awad who might be able to provide us with an Islamic viewpoint on this event. Mr. Ibrahim Awad good morning and welcome to the CXN coverage of this extraordinary event. Can you tell us how you and perhaps Muslim people here in the states and around the world might view this event?"

"Good morning to you all and to all of your viewers throughout the world. Yes I have been in touch with many of my colleagues here this morning in Washington D.C. through a conference call and we are unanimous in our judgement of this event that this is not the Day of Resurrection or the coming of Allah to judge the world, no, that would be a preposterous thing to say in our view. We do believe, of course, that God is great and that Allah will come to the world in an unknown time and pass judgement on all people for their good works and the things they have done wrong also, but we believe that Allah would not return in this way. So we say to Muslim people everywhere that we do not yet have an opinion about who these beings are and we will need to wait until the President returns to address the world, but we expect the return of Allah to be quite different to this. We do not anticipate that Allah will return in some type of spacecraft this way."

"Thank you Mr. Ibrahim Awad for stating that so clearly and perspicuously I am sure that Muslim people all over the world will be greatly relieved to hear that from you, but can you now elaborate on how you do expect Allah to return for the final judgement of people."

"Yes that is no problem, Ms. Foster - we believe that Allah presides over Jannah or the eternal paradise of Heaven and that when Allah does come he will do so with his armies of angels led by the angel Gabriel, from whom the holy Qur'an was given unto our Prophet Mohammed. For it is written in the holy Qur'an that only God knows his armies and truths. So the heavens above will open and there will be trumpets and clouds of brightly colored lights and angels that number so many as to completely cover the sky, some in chariots drawn by horses and unicorn, but all with wings. Before Allah will appear all of the great prophets - Noah, Abraham, Moses, Jesus and the Prophet Mohammed. We believe this will be a great day for all Muslim people and for all good people too, for this will be the Day of Resurrection to eternal life with Allah."

"Just allow me to clarify what you have just said please Mr. Awad. Did you just say that you believe that good people who are not Muslim people will be granted a place in heaven?"

"Yes Mr. Lowry we do believe so, even though the holy Qur'an refers to people who believe in Jesus as God as blasphemers, we now regard this as understandable given the context of the holy Gospel and that Allah will not banish good people for their ignorance or their blasphemy but will judge all people according to their actions."

"That is very encouraging to hear you say that Mr. Ibrahim Awad, I wasn't aware that Islam had, perhaps, moved on into that direction of tolerance toward non-Muslim people, so perhaps we need to do more to communicate that to the people of the world, especially in view of today's events here in New York. But can you tell us whether you do have any hypotheses or theories about who these alien beings might be or where they come from."

"Yes Ms. Foster, it is only my own belief and that of some of my colleagues but we believe that we are being blessed by Allah here today, in some way for Allah watches over us and Allah will intervene in our lives to help us through our troubles. For in the holy Qur'an it is written that God has created many worlds and many universes and it is also written that God has created other beings. So we are hoping to receive some blessings from this visitation somehow. This spacecraft must surely come from another part of the universe because no nation here on earth has the technology to do what their spacecraft has done here today. But they probably do come from somewhere within our own galaxy, for we too understand now how vast the universe is and how vast our galaxy is also."

"Well let's all hope so, Mr. Ibrahim Awad thank you so very much for sharing that with us here this morning I am sure that a lot of people will find considerable comfort in what you have shared with us today."

"Thank you Ms. Foster."

"Well that certainly is re-assuring to me as I was actually feeling a little apprehensive about the Islamic response to this and with what a leader of the Islamic community here in America might have to say, given the level of consternation that has occurred in the world in recent years. But also, because I must admit I really had no idea what to expect from them because we just don't hear from them on quasi-scientific speculation about the universe or E.T. or anything like that."

"Well, Barbara that's possibly because we don't listen to them as much as we should, but perhaps that, too, might change for the better today."

"Yes Professor Jones I certainly hope so. Now we have not yet been able to raise Dr. David Attenborough but we do have our very own eminent biologist Dr. Valmai Green on-line now. Dr. Green is, of course, the director of the Museum of Life Sciences here in Washington in the United States. Dr. Green thank you for joining us."

"Thank you, Barbara, Tom, Alex, Professor."

"Dr. Green, I hope you were tuned in when the President delivered his second rendition here not long ago with some vivid details about life forms on other planets as conveyed to him by visitors."

"Yes, Barbara, I was and I have to say I was absolutely thrilled with what he had to say, about the diversity of life forms and how some that do resemble life forms here on earth can be so similar but also so dissimilar too, but I must admit some of the detail has made me so excited, especially that giant T-Rex and those spiders but those tiny mammals too."

"Are you surprised by what you have heard so far?"

"No I have got to say that when it comes to life and the diversity of forms of life then nothing would surprise me, after all, we just have to look at the diversity of life on earth, historically speaking, to gain an appreciation of the ways that life evolves in every direction imaginable. We know that life forms on earth started from the simplest forms, in fact, that animal life seems to have evolved from the simplest forms of plant life billions of years ago and when you consider all of the variant forms of megafauna that have become extinct over hundreds of millions of years, well I can appreciate that life will evolve in virtually every direction."

"Of course everybody is familiar with our reptilian dinosaur ancestors but if you take more recent history in a place like Australia where so many species of mammal evolved and many extinct species truly were megafauna, like wombats the size of a rhinoceros and even today those two anomalies the platypus and the echidna - well we shouldn't be at all surprised if dinosaurs have evolved with six legs. As for those carnivorous plants that eat animals the size of lions, I have to say - never in my wildest dreams. Now that is something that I do have to see for myself."

"There was once a presentation by Sir David Attenborough where he expressed quite lucidly that every species alive on the planet today is the successful survivor of a long lineage of ancestors that included numerous sub-species that did not survive. I can appreciate that the nature of the gene pool is that it is constantly amorphous and in every generation there are compounding individual differences and in the process of natural selection and survival of the fittest, Mother Nature selects less competitive individuals for culling and those with traits most suitable for survival will breed offspring. So life will evolve in so many different directions depending on the environment and obviously there is a vast array of different environments out there in all of those planets, my God, I am just so excited by all of this. I just hope they can somehow provide us with the natural history of those planets to marvel at. This would be a whole new world for me and everybody in the natural sciences."

"One of the most disappointing aspects of being a natural scientist is knowing of all the hundreds of exotic species of animal that have become extinct here on our own planet, especially since the advent of us, Homo sapiens who have done so much to change the ecology in so many places. We have seen the extinction of the woolly mammoth, the saber-toothed tiger, the dodo bird ... ah ... the Tasmanian thylacine perhaps better known as the Tasmanian tiger, even though it was a marsupial and not a tiger and so many others. So to have an opportunity, at least I hope we do, to see new life forms that have not been adulterated by human intervention is going to be every dream come true for scientists everywhere. So I just hope they can accommodate that somehow, perhaps with visual footage from some distant planets."

"Well they have told us so many amazing things already let's certainly hope that they can share that with us somehow. That certainly would be amazing to see some of those things. Dr. Green thank you for joining us here this morning."

"Thank you, Barbara."

"And that was Dr. Valmai Green from the Washington Museum of Life Sciences."

"We are going to go back now to our man in the street our reporter George Bowman who is still there in the vicinity of the United Nations building and still there is an enormous crowd now in that area. You can see there that thousands of people are milling around talking to each other with some laughing and cheering but also many who seem to be quite mystified by all of this."

"George what can you tell us about the mood down there at the scene, are people expressing their concern at the days unfolding events or are people still quite excited about all of this?"

"Well, Barbara, as you could expect we do have quite a range of emotions being expressed here and ... ah ... I've been on the receiving end of the whole range of responses with some saying this is the greatest thing that has ever happened and others saying it is the end of life as we knew it. I'll just ... ah ... ask this young man what he is thinking right now. Excuse me sir, can you tell us what you make of all of this today."

"I think it's fantastic, you know, until now I have been believing that we might be alone in the universe but, hey, I don't feel so lonely any more, you know, we do have company and I reckon they just might be able to be of assistance to us because, let's face it, we ... ah ... we make quite a lot of trouble for ourselves don't we?"

By now a couple of other people had approached the reporter hoping to have their say.

"And you miss, what do you think about this?"

"Oh look the jury is still out for me because, you know, this could be a ploy because if they did come here to be violent or to plunder they would want to lull us into a false sense of security first, so I am going to reserve my judgement on this for now."

"And you sir, what do you think?"

"I'll tell you what I think, what I've known all along – Jesus was a fraud."

"That might be a bit of a sweeping statement don't you think."

"Well, honestly, how can you reconcile belief in Jesus Christ as God as so many people do when, obviously, these aliens were civilized long before Jesus Christ walked the earth here you know. I mean this really blows all religion clean out of the water. There is no God, just aliens, man."

"And you, miss, what do you think?"

"Yeah look I think it would be really cool if they could kinda impart onto us some of their technology - that is what I am hoping for because we have stuffed up our planet so badly that we are probably gonna need their help to put it right or to be able to colonize some other planet somewhere. It would take us such as long time to work it out for ourselves, how to travel to other planets so I think they could give us quite a leg up with that."

"Well Barbara, there you have it, some of the feelings and views of the people in the street down here and ...ah... I've got to say I hope the positive people prove to be right on this."

"Thank you George Bowman our reporter there still mingling with the very substantial crowd down there outside the UN building and one person has expressed his take on the implications for the world's religions, that Jesus was perhaps not who he is made out to be. So perhaps we need to pursue some more input from some learned people on this very vexed question now."

Chapter 9

Having dwelt on the amazing depictions of exoplanets that abound in the Milky Way Galaxy, as portrayed by the Zircons, the CXN studio presenters took the opportunity to return to their discussions pertaining to the world's religious beliefs with their studio guest Professor David Jones of Notre Dame University.

"Professor Jones just before the President made this second announcement we were about to talk of the Catholic disposition towards other major religions like Islam and Hinduism and how that differs from the Protestant view, can you tell us please where the fundamental differences lay."

"Yes thank you Barbara. Essentially nowadays the Catholic Church does not preach that only Christians are to be "saved and go to heaven" (here he motions italics with his fingertips). Even though the official Catholic Catechism still refers to baptism by water as being virtually a pre-requisite for salvation, modern day theology advances well ahead of amendments to the official Catechism. Of course some major non-Christian religions also baptize with water without acknowledging Jesus as God, which does place them at loggerheads with some Christian churches, but these days there is far more liberal interpretation, even at the grass roots level in the Catholic Church, with the official teachings upheld by Rome. Most Catholic priests, for example, would have no problem whatsoever in teaching that people of all major religions will receive the salvation that Jesus has earned for humanity by his death and resurrection, providing they live their lives as good people. This comes through quite strongly in the Catholic concept of the 'anonymous Christian', which is a relatively recent doctrine dating from the Vatican II period."

Consider this fundamental tenet of the sociology of religion. Of people who are raised by their parents into some form of religious identity, be they Christian or Muslim or Hindu or whatever, throughout the course of their life more than ninety nine percent of those people will retain that same identity, that is, a very small percentage will actually change their fundamental identity or jump ship, if you like, to a different spiritual identity. So very few people raised into Christendom will become Muslim or Buddhist etcetera and within Islam even fewer, because officially Islam forbids such as thing. We see the same in relation to political identity where parents pass on the identity as Republican or Democrat to their children and to a lesser extent in sport and with things like cars – Redsocks versus Cowboys, Ford versus Chrysler etcetera."

"So it is absolute folly to think than an almighty deity who created the universe is going to banish either all Christian people or all Muslim people for eternity, by virtue of the historical and geographical situation into which they were born and over which they had no control. So why all of this consternation within dogmatic religious sects pertaining to people on the other side so to speak? It just doesn't make sense and actually detracts from the true message that they ought to be preaching."

"And that is?"

"That is that God is love. The fundamentalists ought to give up on all of this hellfire and damnation rhetoric and the feelings of spite toward people of alternative beliefs."

"Yes that sounds like very good advice to me."

"Another fundamental tenet of the sociology of religion is that if God did not exist society would create him. This is for the purpose of exercising control over its people – a way of getting into their minds and being able to exercise some form of constraint on what might otherwise be anarchy and total chaos."

"The World Survey on religious beliefs, for example, ascertained that about ninety-five per cent of people in Indonesia professed that religion plays a major role in their life, whereas in China that percentage was only three percent. That result may be slightly skewed by definition because a very high portion of Chinese people do subscribe to the philosophies of Confucianism, which is not actually regarded as a religion per se because it does not acknowledge any deity. But for all intents and purposes Confucianism is a moral code or a religion without a God. Apart from that China has its dictatorial government and military to exercise strict control over its people."

"If you want an insight into the role of religion in higher society and the extent of angst it can create, you would simply need to look no further than, perhaps, Christian people who belong to The Church of Jesus Christ of Latter Day Saints or sometimes better known as the Mormon Church. This church was conceived, of course, by Joseph Smith who wrote the Book of Mormon claiming to have been inspired to do so by God - and well he might have been. I am not here to cast judgement on that although many literary analysts have concluded that it is purely the work of a man rather than being a work of divine inspiration, but some literary scholars postulate the same of the holy Qur'an. As we all know Salt Lake City in Utah is where the church is centered and we are all familiar with some of the extraordinary aspects of that faith, notably that young Mormon people are virtually required by their community to undertake two years of missionary work and that is usually in an overseas location. So they go overseas for two years and they live or board with a family of their faith or otherwise and they receive financial support from their community back home in the states but they do live a very frugal life while they are away, which forbids the consumption of alcohol, tobacco, tea or coffee. Their role is to talk to people to try to bring people closer to God, hopefully through their own church."

"Yes and I believe there could be some sanctions for those who don't undertake the missionary work."

"Well Barbara, if you need a more cogent example of the power of religion in society you need to look no further, for theirs is a classical case. Anybody who wants to be somebody within Salt Lake City with any large corporation or employer, such as a law firm or top accounting firm or an information technology company, had better have that missionary credential on their curriculum vitae or they don't stand a chance. If you have not completed your missionary work don't even bother applying for most jobs. In fact most young people who shun that missionary requirement leave Salt Lake City for that reason and for other reasons too – the general stigma associated with not having completed the two years of missionary work. That stigma is felt from within their own family and relatives, within their network of close friends and now, of course, even the wider community because of Facebook and other social networking media. So the word gets around. The unfortunate aspect of that is it goes against the United Nations charter on individual freedoms – which picks up freedom of religious expression. Those people ought to be free to choose their own spiritual beliefs without that level of social coercion."

"Yes I have a friend who applied for a position as an electrical engineer in Salt Lake City and when he went for the interview the very first question they asked him was whether or not he was a Mormon."

"Which is not surprising Tom, but it is also a known fact that in the general corporate world religious people who permeate their way toward the top tend to show a bias in selection processes for employment or promotion, to people of their ilk. They will quite often advertise for new employees via church websites before any other medium, knowing that they can possibly recruit a fellow Christian. Even then, Protestant Christians will show bias toward fellow Protestants rather than Catholics."

"Why would they do that?"

"They do that because, apart from the natural human tendency to favor one's own, there is an underlying animosity that fundamentalist Protestant churches feel toward the Catholic Church, which is something that is nurtured by their preachers. After all, the Catholic Church upholds itself as the 'mother church' and refutes the notion that Protestant churches are in any way 'sister churches'. Pope Benedict XVI incurred the wrath of American Protestants by reiterating that policy when he was a Cardinal and his proclamation was endorsed by the, then, Pontiff - Pope John Paul II."

"Some Protestant preachers promulgate false information about the Catholic Church for the same reason. I became aware that many Assembly of God churches were informing their congregations that Catholics believe that Mary is God. There would not actually be a single Catholic person in the entire world who believes that Mary is God. More widespread is the practice of denigrating the Catholic Church for its supposed worship of statues and some other peculiar practices that might be regarded by them as decadent – such as the Rosary and Benediction. But such things are parts of cultural expression and a lot of Catholics are people who like to uphold age-old traditions and we should not think less of them for that because many of those traditions date back many centuries. You could say the Sacrament of Communion, for example, dates back to The Last Supper of Jesus with his disciples."

"I have actually heard things like that for myself when I went to a Pentecostal church with an old girlfriend many years ago – the preacher made several derogatory remarks about the Catholic Church's worship of statues etcetera."

"Yes Tom, there is quite a substantial degree of 'us and them' even within Christian circles and it's just so unfortunate that this spills over into doctrine pertaining to eternal salvation. So try to imagine the extent of this among conservative Christians toward Muslim people."

"Yes, that does seem to be quite bereft of love, charity and compassion now doesn't it?"

"So Professor Jones, how do you as a practicing Catholic reconcile your own rather liberal views on questions of theology with the official teachings of your own Catholic Church on issues such as Papal infallibility and certain aspects of sexuality, such as de-facto marriage or even gay marriage?"

"Well I profess to be what is known as a modern day Catholic, so I am more inclined to use my own judgement on such things than a traditional Catholic person would. I do not pray to Mary and I do believe that all people who believe in God belong to one church here on earth, regardless of their denomination or whether they are Muslim or Hindu or whatever. As a modern day Catholic I observe most of the church's teaching, but I use my own mind on a lot of issues where I believe the church needs to update."

"So apart from the question of papal infallibility and questions pertaining to sexuality where does the modern day Catholic as you call yourself differ in belief from the authority in Rome?"

"Well certainly in respect of a lot of what I would call decadent ritualism that lingers and prevails within the Catholic Church. Of course as an academic I do understand that a lot of the bells and whistles of pomp and ceremony have a significant role in authenticating the belief system. It

137

wouldn't look right, for example, if your average Catholic priest celebrated the holy Mass in a pair of football shorts and a t-shirt, so the adornment of the chasuble is conducive to authenticating the ceremony and the meaning therein. But we see that also in our police forces, our military establishments and indeed in the corporate world too, the adornment of a uniform standard of dress speaks to people and confirms credibility. But on the other hand that celebration of the holy Mass comes with so many other trimmings too, like the candles and flowers, the gen-reflection and the striking of the breast and sometimes they spray the people with holy water. So that type of external symbolism doesn't always gel well with people of a rational mindset and as a professional person I am no exception to that. What I would regard as the silliness of the ceremony."

"And Professor you mentioned Purgatory and Limbo before. How do the Protestant churches account for such theology?"

"The theology of Purgatory and Limbo is accepted by mainstream Protestant churches, but the fundamentalist churches that do not accept that doctrine, simply explain away all of those paradoxes we talked about earlier - such as the still born child. That includes, of course, most of those in the Pentecostal movement. They don't have a problem with such inscrutable questions because, once again, they can refer to scripture to justify that such persons were not meant to be saved. Take for example where Jesus said 'I chose you, you did not choose me'. When you arm yourself with enough scriptural verse, you can virtually explain away anything."

"That seems a little harsh to believe that a stillborn child would not be saved to heaven, do they really believe that?"

"Well yes they do because they take a very literal interpretation of the scripture and the stillborn child has not been baptized nor 'born again' or pray in tongues so the

Pentecostals simply put the eternal fate of that unfortunate child down to the will of God."

"So Professor tell us more about this phenomenon that you refer to here that seems to be so central to the beliefs of Pentecostal Christians – they believe that in order to be 'saved' as they put it, which I take to mean that a person dies and goes to heaven – you have to be born again and to pray in tongues. Is that right?"

"Yes that belief is true of perhaps the vast majority of Assembly of God Christians and to a far lesser extent other Pentecostal Protestants and Catholics who do not come in for the same level of extreme indoctrination as their Assembly of God counterparts, but within Assembly of God circles, yes, they certainly do promulgate a very literal interpretation of the Gospel, where Jesus said you cannot go to Heaven unless you are born again."

"Well that all seems very strange that Jesus would say something like that considering that most of us here in the states have at least an inkling of what it means to be so-called 'born again'. We see their conventions on television and we know, for example, that people who are born again refer to being baptized in the Spirit, that Jesus is their personal Lord and savior and that they claim to receive gifts like prophecy or healing. And of course, there is all of the fervor and zeal that they display when they do come together for a church service – you have to give them that they are certainly enamored with the Lord. But did Jesus really say this is the way we all have to be?"

"No Barbara! It is fundamentally a question of interpretation. I don't question that Jesus said we must be born again as that is recorded in the Gospel, but the question is what did he mean? Did he mean that you must go through all of those things you have just described that the Pentecostal people experience? No! He did not! This is a matter of

Pentecostal Christians falsely attributing those words of Jesus Christ, to their own experience, to where they are in their relationship with him. His real meaning is something that is open for contemplation and has been for scholars for hundreds of years but the relatively recent trend of Pentecostal Christians to attribute their experience of God, that total commitment to God, with what Jesus, himself, referred to as being born again, is false. Basically, that is not what Jesus meant at all."

"I am glad to hear you say that Professor Jones because my sister is a regular at her local Baptist church and there are Pentecostal people there who told her that unless she becomes born again and prays in tongues she will not be received in heaven when she departs this world, which seems very harsh to me because she has always been a devout Christian and is a truly wonderful person."

"Yes that is not surprising, Barbara, the extreme dogmatists within the Pentecostal movement do preach such things and that is very unfortunate, of course, and does cause quite some consternation within their own church groups, like the Baptist church or the Church of Christ or the United Methodist Church, for example."

"So tell us about the misinterpretation if you will."

"Okay, Tom, as I stated earlier the question of what Jesus meant has intrigued theologians ever since the day and there are various and wide-ranging meanings that have been attributed to his words. What is far easier to quantify is what the Pentecostal people understand by his words and that is, essentially, they attribute their experience in giving their lives whole heartedly to God and being baptized in the spirit to being born again. They think this is what Jesus meant when he said you must be born again."

"And why do they think that?"

"Because somebody told them to!"

"Ah ... can it really be that simple?"

"Yes! This is the power of socialization. I am a sociologist so I understand how this process works better than most people would, but it really is testimony to that power of socialization. Somebody, quite some time ago decided that this experience of total commitment to the Lord that the Pentecostal people - and others – have decided for themselves, is what Jesus meant when he said you must be born again. It is not difficult to understand or appreciate how this would catch on. It seems totally credible to them. Unfortunately they have a tendency to then regard other people, even very devout Christian people such as Barbara's sister, with a degree of disdain or even contempt – they regard such people as not being born again and therefore not being saved."

"And the implication of that is?"

"To them that means eternity in hell and they do believe in hell as a place of eternal punishment. Some still believe it is a place where a fire is burning. Literally!"

"Are you for real? They think that my sister who is the best person I have ever known and I, myself, are going to burn for eternity in a fire in hell? I am not sure that I would want to know that God."

"Yes, it seems that the more extreme dogmatists, certainly in the Pentecostal movement, do believe that. But they are not the only ones, of course, it is quite a common belief among cultist religious factions and ultra conservative Christian movements, like the Jehovah's Witnesses, perhaps to a lesser extent Latter Day Saints but now also the Assembly of God."

"Of course, I have mentioned the Jehovah's Witnesses there – they are not Pentecostal Christians - but they do believe everybody but themselves are doomed to some form of eternal punishment or non-existence. We also see the same

141

type of dogmatism among extremists in Islam, for example, who make reference to all non-Islamic people being infidel."

"Okay, so that quantifies what Pentecostal Christians and certain others think. So what do the theologians think about this meaning of being born again?"

"As I said their interpretations are wide and varied and perhaps center on two things. One that Jesus meant you must be prepared to surrender your basic human nature that is intrinsically, well, perhaps not evil but, Godless, and to turn back toward God from where we came before our original sin. We don't have any idea what that sin was except for its metaphorical portrayal in the book of Genesis in the story of Adam and Eve..."

"Which is something that the Pentecostal Christians believe in, literally – Adam and Eve, I mean!"

"Yes, they do for the purpose of saying they believe in the Bible! But whatever we did we turned away from God and so were banished to live this life as our second chance to move back toward him."

"Or perhaps our third chance or our fourth chance or our tenth chance?"

"As explained within Hinduism, yes, hundreds of millions of people around the world do subscribe fully to the concept of reincarnation as a progression of lives moving closer to – or even further away from – God. But we might have to come back to that later, Alex. In fact I have a large number of modern day Catholic friends who are very learned people – lawyers, philosophers, mathematicians, physicists – who do subscribe to the concept of reincarnation. Why? Because it really is the only thing that makes much sense at all."

"And the second thing?"

"This follows on from the first – that we are required to live a life of goodness and, essentially, to live according to the golden rule – to do unto others as you would have them do unto you. The golden rule is ensconced within every major spiritual philosophy – obviously within the ancient Jewish scripture, within the Dharmic religions of Buddhism and Hinduism, within Confucianism and Taoism and within the Qur'an. Of course, Jesus gave a new dimension to the golden rule with his Great Commandment – that he said you must love your neighbor as yourself."

"So is this where the majority of Catholic theologians are today, that they believe when Jesus said you must be born again he meant to love your neighbor as yourself?"

"Yes, Barbara, absolutely!"

"Boy am I glad to hear you say that. So my sister is safe, quite safe?"

"Take it from me Barbara, both your sister and yourself have a place in heaven."

"Me? Why me, I don't go to church like she does?"

"You don't have to go to church to be a Christian – or Christ like – person, Barbara. You are Christ like in your profession, you are doing what you do to try to make the world a better place for the sake of other people and that is the type of love that Jesus expects from us."

"And this is the modern-day explanation from theologians of what Jesus meant to be born again?"

"Yes, but not all theologians. You need to understand that many Protestant theologians still uphold a very dogmatic line, but that is partly because some dogmatic Protestants are drawn towards studying theology. Within the parlance of sociology, we refer to 'causal relationships' between variables - so that relationship would be the converse of the norm. I have alluded to the Catholic Church's exposition of the anonymous Christian, even though a lot of good people might object to being referred to as Christians, where they do not practice any overt spirituality, such as yourself, Barbara, nevertheless

Jesus acknowledged that in being good people and loving others we are born again to a new life with God."

"We are hoping to have a representative from the Catholic Church on-line soon so perhaps we can ask for some kind of endorsement of that perspective when the time comes. Professor Jones, is there a scriptural basis for what seems to be a very broad interpretation of what it means to be born again that you have just espoused here and what do you think the Pentecostals would think about that?"

"Yes there is and when your Catholic guest comes on later may I suggest you seek the views of the Catholic Church on that, but also conventional non-fundamentalist theology considers the response of Jesus to the rich young man as being the scriptural basis for this. The rich young man put the question to Jesus 'Lord what must I do to enter the kingdom of Heaven?' and Jesus gave him a very straightforward answer."

"Which was?"

"Follow the Ten Commandments!"

"In other words - be a good person?"

"Yes, Jesus went on to say that his new commandment, to love your neighbor as yourself, is the meaning of the Ten Commandments and the teaching of the prophets."

"And what would the Pentecostals think about this?"

"They don't accept this interpretation and they get rather perturbed to think that God's salvation would extend to so many billions of good people in the world when they regard themselves as being somewhat privy to the Kingdom of God. Just last week I was watching some historical footage of Pastor Benny Hinn saying things like 'you cannot be saved through the prophet Mohammed, you cannot be saved through reincarnation - you can only be saved through Jesus' and he believes that and so do his followers. What they need to take heed of really is what Jesus then said to the rich young

man – that if you want to be perfect come and follow me. That is where the Pentecostal people are."

"Ah … right … now that makes sense, they are living their lives closer to the Lord that all of us ordinary mundane Christians."

Everybody chuckled.

"Yes, Barbara you have hit the nail on the head with that one, the Pentecostal Christians literally fall in love with Jesus and who can blame them, they are typically overwhelmed by the very powerful things that Jesus said."

"Such as?"

"The things that Jesus said - where do I start? I am the vine and you are the branches, I am the way, the truth and the life, turn the other cheek, love your enemies, the parable of the Good Shepherd – when you wander away from him he will come looking for you; the parable of the Prodigal Son – if you return to God he will hug you and kiss you and bless you with a banquet; the parable of the vineyard workers - it is never too late to turn to God - he will always be waiting for you; the parable of the Good Samaritan – everybody is your neighbor, not just your fellow Christians or fellow Muslim people; the Sermon on the Mount – blessed are the kind and merciful, blessed are they who hunger and thirst after justice, blessed are the meek. There are so many really significant utterances of Jesus that totally personify love of neighbor and give people reason to follow him closely, that the proclivity of Pentecostal Christians to regard us lesser Christians with a degree of disdain is actually quite understandable – not justifiable but nevertheless understandable."

"So they choose to live their lives as close to Jesus as possible?"

"Yes and that is what the good Lord said to the rich young man who expressed that he felt he needed more than to simply be a good person. He was reaching out to the Lord for

spiritual perfection and Jesus challenged him by saying that if he, the rich young man, wanted to be perfect he would have to surrender his existing life and to follow Jesus."

"And that is where the Pentecostals are – living their lives close to Jesus."

"Yes but it is unfortunate that they become so dogmatic in the process but that really is a matter of education. You see they are typically educated into dogmatism by their elders, who themselves either fail to understand the broader interpretations of scripture or may have some other ulterior motive."

"Such as?"

"Such as money, or power, or ego or vanity!"

"Ah hah ... I think we know where you are heading with this, that they demand money from their followers in the form of ... ah ... what do they call it again?"

"Tithings!"

"Yes is it ten percent of their income?"

"Ten percent of their gross income – not their net income!"

"That adds up to a lot of money over a period of time."

It is an enormous amount of money and for many people, if not most, it would mean the difference between having security in their lives or being close to destitute and never owning their own home."

"So why do people accede on this, why do they part with their money so freely?"

"Fundamentally there are three reasons, the first being the social coercion that exists from others within the church, the people who are tithers will encourage or cajole newcomers into donating a tenth of their income as if that is what the Lord himself requires. Secondly, what is so often concomitant with that is the fear of damnation – that newcomers are initially cajoled but subsequently are in fact coerced into tithings for fear of eternal damnation."

"Surely God wouldn't damn somebody for eternity for not being a tither?"

"No of course he would not but that doesn't stop lay preachers whose own livelihood and income depends on there being a lot of tithers within their church, from telling people that God will damn them for eternity if they don't give their ten percent."

"And the third reason?"

"Prosperity doctrine! Again I refer to Pastor Benny Hinn who said it quite plainly – 'God wants you to be wealthy and how can I preach that to you if I, myself, am poor'. So he ensures that he becomes very wealthy from preaching the word of God so as to not be seen as hypocritical."

"Sounds more like a rationalization of theft to me!"

"Alex, there are many who agree with you and, of course, in order to receive the wealth that God has seemingly promised, one has to give the ten per cent or forfeit one's promise of wealth."

"So God will not bestow this wealth upon non-tithers?"

"That is exactly the form the coercion takes. Of course, in recent times we have witnessed Iowa Senator Chuck Grassley and his Congressional Committee take some of these people on and bring them to account for the wealth they themselves have usurped in the process. Of course one of Senator Grassley's main points of interest in this pertained to the, the ... ah ... very generous taxation concessions afforded by Inland Revenue to these churches. The pastors themselves are really quite notorious for building mansions and buying private jets but not necessarily paying their share of taxes."

"Which they can justify because they are doing the Lord's work."

"Yes in fact it was quite some time ago as I recall, perhaps even back in the sixty's, that Pastor Billy Graham, who was extremely popular at the time, responded to a question from a journalist asking why he drove a Rolls Royce and his response was that he was a tradesman for the Lord and, as such, he needed the best tools."

"Well that's a classical rationalization if ever I heard one."

"Oh some do much better than that Tom. A Rolls Royce was a minor expense compared to an eleven-million-dollar jet."

"Didn't Creflo Dollar buy a sixty-million-dollar jet?"

"Yes I believe somebody funded that for him."

"And the justification for the jet?"

"Jets! They all have one now! If you are going to do the Lord's work with total efficiency you cannot allow yourself to be caught up at airports waiting for domestic flights, or international flights, by the conventional airlines. The delays, in fact, could be regarded by the Lord himself as being sinful, considering that there are so many souls out there waiting to be saved. No - you must have your own jet for efficiency if you are going to save those extra souls."

"Hmmm ... and what does your Catholic Church think about this Professor Jones?"

"As I said before, Barbara, the Catholic Church will not place people under that type of duress and promotes the verse from Saint Paul to the Corinthians that each man should give according to his conscience for God loves a cheerful giver."

"I am willing to play the devil's advocate here for a moment so just let me get my head around some figures here, as best I know there are millions of Americans now in the Assembly of God and if you were an aspiring preacher and were going to procure ten per cent from everybody who joins your church, you wouldn't actually need that many to make a good living for yourself – dare I say – ten."

"Don't overlook other costs Alex. To be a preacher you need premises, you need some admin staff and various support personnel but yes you could start up your own church by bringing in just a couple of hundred people, for sure."

"Which might account for why we have seen this proliferation of AOG churches popping up virtually everywhere, especially in industrial estates or commercial areas, where they tend to lease what is essentially a factory of some kind."

"Yes, Tom, a lot of them will break away from a larger group when that group is starting to reach saturation point and someone who thinks he or she can preach a good message will break off and lease some premises, then typically start offering select people an income to work for him or her and that's when the business decisions start to take hold – if I pay more to my promoters rather than less, they will bring in even more worshippers. So now there are more fulltime preachers in the states working for AOG that there are priests and pastors in all other churches – some three hundred and fifty thousand of them."

"And I am wondering if there are any inducements on offer for people to recruit new church members, I mean, if every new person donates ten per cent of their gross income that leaves a lot of scope for recruitment rewards to be offered for a time."

"Well Alex in some places the recruitment process does resemble those that are adopted by network marketing corporations and we do have better than anecdotal evidence of inducements being offered to people to recruit, yes."

"So this can become big business, then?"

"Alex, in the United States of America, religion has become huge business, because of tithings. But the protagonists don't have any compunction nor too many qualms about their activities nor how they remunerate themselves because they are saving souls for the Lord."

"And what of the dogmatism in all of this – this dogma that you have to be a born again Christian to enter the Kingdom of Heaven and, overtly Christian, is that how I read it – you can't be half-baked about this!"

"A cynic might suggest that there is not as much money in a half-baked Christian so it would be in the best interests of the leaders in a church to engender and to nurture a rather vehement culture towards commitment to Jesus. But on the question of the dogmatism, per se, I should introduce my associate here at the university Dr. Belinda Bates who is undertaking her post doctorate studies now in this very field of dogmatism in religion."

"Hey Dr. Bates, welcome to CXN on this very special day and let me say how interesting we have found it to listen to the professor shed some light on what we have been hearing here today from some of our leaders of religion, some of which could only be described as peculiar. I hope you can enlighten us some more."

"Thank you Barbara, I certainly hope so. Let me begin just by stating that my interest in this emanates from what I perceive as a universal problem, now that extremism and cultism in religious ideology really has its roots firmly set in dogmatism, which I should define, for the sake of your listeners, as 'an unreasoned hard line belief that fails to accommodate any form of dissension' - although definitions are wide and varied but these are the two essential aspects of dogmatism. So my area of study is in relation to dogmatism in both Christianity and in Islam, because to me these are the two major religious belief systems in the world today where dogmatism is a powerful force and one that polarizes people to a great extent against the other."

"If you think dogmatism is not significant then consider that the people who are causing massive problems around the world today with their extreme views, of Islam in particular, are a product of hard-core socialization and indoctrination that is totally intolerant of any other belief and for this they are prepared to commit horrific acts of murder and even of genocide. Their motives are fundamentally political, but they rationalize or justify their actions with exhortations to Islam."

"So take it from me that dogmatism is alive and well in every religious belief system, but in some sectors within a system more than others. If you take Islam for example dogmatism is very readily identifiable and the politically extremist clerics will espouse jihad or holy war against any non-Islamic person. I have to add here that many of these so-called clerics are self-appointed – they don't actually have to undergo any form of training or attain a formal qualification to put themselves out there as a cleric. So when I refer to them as Islamic I don't mean that they are genuinely Muslim, but that they do believe they are."

"Why would you not regard them as Muslim people if they believe they are and they certainly make exhortations to Islam?"

"I differentiate for two reasons Alex. Firstly, they were definitely raised as Muslim people - that is the common situation - they were raised into Islam but there comes a point when a person's actions defy the belief system they supposedly subscribe to. Secondly, on this I have a saying that 'hypocrisy abrogates belief', hypocrisy repeals or cancels out a belief, so you can't profess to be a Christian person and take a gun down to your local bank and murder somebody and steal the banks money, as much as one might like to think of themselves as a Christian or Muslim person. To resort to acts that blatantly contravene the belief system does abrogate or repeal one's claim to be a believer."

"Consider that more than half the long-term prisoners in American prisons were raised into a Christian family – Catholic, Anglican, Baptist, Methodist, Mormon, Jehovah and so on, but they made their own personal decision to do whatever wrong they did and to abrogate their Christian belief of 'love your neighbor as yourself'. It is no different with terrorists who were raised into Islam and made their decision to resort to violence toward a political end, but in doing so they literally cease to be Muslim people."

"So the extremists that we see in the world today who supposedly subscribe to Islam and who perpetrate acts of terror on innocent people will encourage violence against people they regard as infidel and to any dissident of Islam. They will even declare a fatwa upon the head of a person who speaks out against them, as we saw with Salman Rushdie after he published his book 'The Satanic Verses'. As best I recall that fatwa was declared by the Ayatollah Khomeini the elected leader in Iran at the time."

"Even more relevant is perhaps the incidence of suicide bombings and the mass murder of innocent people, especially westerners, as a result of some misguided vendetta against western culture or western society. But always it is people at the top dictating to virtual pawns below them that they need to perpetrate these horrific acts as a means of martyrdom and eternal life in paradise. So this is one of the key elements in dogmatism - it emanates from the top and permeates its way downward to the rank and file. It is also very commonplace for the people who do promulgate dogmatic views to have an ulterior motive as, I believe, the professor has covered to some extent."

"The real motives of jihadist Islamic terrorists are the pursuit of political power and the wealth that comes with that, which includes pillaging and plundering, they do enjoy violence and taking up arms to engage in war-like conflict and they are prepared to sexually exploit and abuse women – and that includes rape. The rape of women and children, of girls as young as eight years of age, has been reliably reported in the media and those reports have come from the Red Cross and various missionary organizations, such as World Vision and Save the Children. We are also aware that in recruiting young men from western countries the terrorists have placed some emphasis on sexual gratification as part of the spoils of war. As one so-called cleric put it quite lucidly – 'you will get laid'. A lot of those young men would have never experienced any kind of sexual relationship because of that being taboo within their family community. Now we know that hundreds, perhaps even thousands, of women who were taken as sex slaves and forced into pregnancy were also forced into having abortions."

"So those jihadist Islamic terrorists are political extremists. Within Islam per se, that is among people who do live a typical good Muslim life, we still see varying degrees of dogmatism at work in the intolerance of large sectors toward any form of dissension. Of course there are more moderate believers in Islam too, who respect the beliefs of others and who do understand others beliefs. After all, the prophet Mohammed does make reference to Jesus in his holy Quran and to Jesus' mother - Mary."

"We do see the same processes at work in Christianity and in Judaism and other religions too. Within the Dharmic religions we see this in Hinduism far more so than any other Dharmic religion, because of the caste system in Hinduism."

"So within Christian churches there are varying degrees of dogmatism, from the hard line very conservative, traditional hellfire and damnation doctrine that persists even today in many Christian churches to a less vehement or more moderate form of dogmatism that is still very conservative but doesn't completely dismiss the beliefs of others."

"But my main area of interest as a psychologist is how and why are the processes of dogmatic preaching accepted so readily by the people who come under its influence."

So have you been able to draw any profound conclusions from your research to date?"

"Oh absolutely, we don't have any problem identifying certain root causes nor in identifying how these can affect people, dare I say afflict people and there is quite a lot of research into this already. There are a number of common traits that are concomitant with dogmatism and these include the upholding of one's beliefs as totally inerrant, a dire lack of understanding of alternative beliefs, hard line intransigence towards any alternative viewpoints, blatant arrogance, autocracy, a minatory or threatening disposition toward any form of apostasy, flagrant disregard of the lives of people who subscribe to any other belief system and my pet area as a psychologist, that they actually feel some degree of malice toward people they regard as being on the other side of the fence."

"So you are talking about hard-line Christians who regard non-Christians with contempt?"

"Yes but apostasy is probably more an issue in Islam rather than in Christianity and the intrinsic aspect of renouncing apostasy in Islam is virtually self-perpetuating. Islamic families educate their children into a profound belief that they must never turn away from Islam to subscribe to any other religion."

"But just as extremists in Islam regard anybody outside of Islam as infidel, the same is true in Christian circles. Traditional conservative Christians and Pentecostals in particular, regard all Muslim people, all Jews, all Buddhists and all Hindus etcetera, as being doomed to eternal damnation. This attitude toward all non-Christians does include a degree of malice – they feel good about themselves and they feel very smug with their life in the Lord and studies have borne out that they even feel somewhat good about knowing that so many others, people on the other side of the fence, will not be saved."

"Why would they feel good about that?"

They do, Tom, because they not only feel good about themselves, but somehow believing that all people who are not born-again Christians are going to be damned actually makes them feel better about themselves. We have one PhD student whose entire research is dedicated to the differentiation between two groups of Christians – one group of born again Pentecostals and the other devout churchgoers - and the research was able to delineate the variable that gave some measure to that – and the line of questioning to determine that variable has passed scrutiny at the top levels of scientific method. The upshot of all that was that the Pentecostals endorsed the doctrine that all Muslim people, for example, would not be saved and that made them feel really good about being a born-again Christian. But the study focused also on body language when this doctrine was put to them. "

"That has been borne out in research studies and to me, I have to say it, that seems to be so totally anathema to what they supposedly believe – love of neighbor as self. I, myself am a churchgoing Anglican so I must be wary of selective perception in my analyses ..."

"Selective perception?"

"Yes that is a moderate form of bias that the protagonist does not or cannot actually realize is a part of them and is intrinsic within all of us in some way, but we do have scientific tests to eradicate such a bias in our studies."

"To me their attitude smacks of the same attitude as the elder brother of the Prodigal Son, who became obsessively envious of his younger brother when the father accepted his son back into his household – the parallel meaning being that the Lord accepted the wayward sinner back into his kingdom. As the father said to his eldest son 'everything I have is yours'.

So Christians ought not to feel envious if Muslim people and others are welcomed into the kingdom of God, but strangely, Pentecostal Christians seem to do just that!"

"Hmm ... yes well thank you for that Dr. Bates, that really is very interesting – the psychology of dogmatism – perhaps some of that research can form the basis of a renaissance in the education of religious beliefs in our high school systems. Our educationists might be able to nurture greater tolerance and understanding."

"Thank you, Barbara!"

"Now we are still some way off from the President's next presentation here so I suppose we might take a short break and take a word from our sponsor and we will see if we can raise another interested party to come online here."

Chapter 10

While the President was being further briefed by the Zircons and CXN had interviewed Dr. Bates, Michael had tried to compose himself as he needed to inform his wife Julie of the tragedy that had unfolded between Chrissy and her husband Graham. Julie was already at her parent's house. Her telephone rang and she knew it was Michael, but she waited for him to talk first.

"Julie..."

Then he fell silent, but she could hear him breathing. She assumed he was feeling remorseful for what he had done, but she just gave him time to get himself together. Then she heard him weeping.

"Michael, I have been talking to my parents. They want me to stay here as long as it takes to finalize everything – the house, everything."

Still Michael continued to weep.

"You must know and understand what my parents think of you now, Michael – they did express their reservations to me when I first met you. They said they would have referred me to meet somebody from our Baptist church."

Michael took a deep breath. He was about to tell Julie about Chrissy having been shot and killed by her husband but this comment from her took him back a few paces. Thoughts raced through his mind.

"So I never had their approval from the start, eh! Well I am not surprised Julie and ... ah ... I can't help but wonder whether that had an effect on you in our marriage - you know. I have always felt their superficial responses to me every time we were together with them. And the comments about me not being baptized in the spirit weren't lost on me either. They probably regarded me as the devil himself."

157

"That's not true Michael! It's just that there are preachers at church who tell them that you are a good man but that you will not be saved."

"Yeah, well ... ah ... we might have to talk about that some other time, Julie, right now I need to let you know that something tragic has happened."

"Something tragic!"

"Yes ... ah ... it seems that when Christine arrived home her husband Graham must have been in a furor – possibly because of what he might have witnessed on television where he was with his workmates. Well he ... ah ... decided to end his life, Julie, but he took it out on Christine before he committed suicide."

"Oh my God, Michael, no! Is Christine okay?"

"I'm afraid not Julie. He took her with him."

Julie's first thought was the impact this would have on her own husband.

"Oh my God! Oh poor Christine! And Graham!"

Julie started to weep but she took a deep breath and tried to collect her thoughts.

"Now Michael, listen to me, this is not your fault, do you hear, this is not your fault Michael. Regardless of what happened Graham had no right to do what he did. He should have sought counselling for them. Michael, do not blame yourself for this, do you hear me Michael. Now where are you?"

"I am back at the house. Julie I feel so terrible, I feel so sick - I can't believe this has happened to Christine, to us. Julie I know I have done the wrong thing. I am so sorry for what I have done to you, to us. I promise I will be a good man forever now."

To Julie these words were like a man repenting before God and, as such, it certainly struck a chord with her. She had heard the same words many times when people repented before her church congregation. This caused Julie to weep even more. She was a good devout Christian woman and her own thoughts now had turned toward her husband. Even though he had been unfaithful to her just the night before, she did not wish any harm upon her husband and she was already thinking of their own reconciliation process. Perhaps she could educe a stronger commitment from her husband, toward herself and toward her God. Perhaps he would recommence attending his church every Sunday the way he used to. That meant everything to her. She also started to worry about what he might do next, should he blame himself for Christine's demise.

"Now Michael you stay right there, okay. I will talk to my parents for a little while and then tell them I need to go somewhere and I will leave the girls here and come to see you. Okay! Just stay there I will be there as soon as I can. I am going to go offline now."

Julie did not want to tell her parents that she was going to see Michael, so she told them she was going out to see a friend.

"Mom, dad, I need to go see a friend now so I will leave the girls with you and I will ... ah ... come back when I can, okay. Now you girls be good for nan and pop. Mommy will be back after dinner."

Julie left her parent's house and drove away in her car in quite a hurry. Too much of a hurry! She was so concerned for Michael that she drove through a 'Give Way' sign just a little too quickly and failed to see the vehicle speeding towards her from her left. The accident was substantial, Julie was injured and had to be cut from the wreckage of her car by the fire and emergency services. She was taken to hospital under heavy sedation. The police called Michael as Julie had an 'ice' number in her telephone.

"Mr. Michael McIntyre?"

"Yes, speaking."

"Mr. McIntyre my name is Sargent Raymond Phillips of the New York Police Department. Your wife is Julie McIntyre?"

"Yes Julie is my wife – why do you ask?"

"Mr. McIntyre your wife Julie is has just been involved in a traffic accident on Devon Promenade and your wife is presently on her way to hospital in an ambulance with some injuries, but we do believe your wife will be fine."

"Oh shit! Not Julie! Can you tell me which hospital she is being taken to?"

"Yes they should be arriving at Saint Vincent's emergency department any time now, so you will find her there. Now it seems that your wife was in quite a hurry, so you take it easy now, you hear."

"Thank you, officer! I will."

Michael's first reaction was one of total shock, but this led him into feeling how much he loved his wife. He then felt that he was to blame for this newest tragedy as he knew Julie would be driving rather quickly on her way to see him for what he had done and because of Chrissy's demise. He thought he was being punished now for his misdemeanors.

Michael then telephoned Julie's parents to inform them of the situation.

"Hello Michael, Julie is not here she left about an hour ago to go see somebody – she didn't say who but ..."

"Yes Vesna I know – Julie was on her way to see me actually but, she is okay but she had ... ah ... she had a little accident on the way and she has been admitted to Saint Vincent's Hospital, but I have been informed that she will be fine, you understand."

"Oh my God! Simon ... Simon, Julie is in hospital she has been involved in an accident. Michael, are you sure our Julie is alright?"

"Yes Vesna she is, I called the hospital and the nurse informed me that Julie's injuries are superficial – a few cuts and some bruises."

"We will go to the hospital now Michael – we will be there as soon as we can."

Julie's mother Vesna telephoned Pastor James to let him know that Julie was in hospital. Pastor James was only about ten minutes from the hospital and would arrive there several minutes before Michael would.

Pastor James was directed to Julie's room. He entered the room where Julie lay awake in the bed, with the television on showing the CXN coverage of the morning's events.

"Julie, oh Julie, thank God you are alright. How terrible! My God look at you Julie – do you have lacerations on your neck?"

"Yes I have been very fortunate James, the doctors said I nearly lacerated an artery."

"It's not like you to be involved in an accident, Julie – you are always so careful. Was the other motorist reckless?"

"No James it was my fault, I was in too much of a hurry to see Michael. I was worried about him. James, there has been a terrible tragedy today – a work associate of Michael's, Christine McMullan, the woman they call Chrissy, has been shot dead by her husband and my Michael ... was feeling guilty for her demise."

"Michael! Why would Michael be feeling any guilt?"

"James ... they were seen on television this morning near the UN building. They were kissing, James. When I confronted Michael about this today, he admitted that last night they had an affair – in the office while he was working back."

"Oh my God Julie, I feel so sorry for you. You must be devastated."

"Yes, James, of course I was, so I packed my belongings and went to my parent's house, but while I was there Michael learned of his friend's demise, so he called me and ... I was worried that he might do something rash so I told him to stay put while I went to see him. That is when I was driving too fast, because I was so worried about losing him."

"Ah ... Julie, you do realize that what Michael has done is so very wrong, so very sinful and ... ah ... of course your husband is now an adulterer, Julie."

"I am not thinking about that right at this moment, James, there has been too much happen today for me to be cognizant of anything at the moment – with the event this morning, seeing Michael on television, then learning about Christine and now my accident."

"But Julie ... this is our chance ... to be together, you and me. Your husband Michael has abrogated his marriage to you Julie. You know how our feelings have been growing for each other in these last few months. This is our chance to be together ... forever."

"James ... what Michael did, it is not all Michael's fault. These last few months with you and me hugging and kissing when sharing the sign of peace, growing closer and closer to each other emotionally, I really have not been there as the good wife to Michael that I should have been. Michael was vulnerable to Christine, who obviously had her own problems with her husband and she took advantage of him James. I might be just as culpable for what he has done James."

"But Julie ... I love you. I really want to be with you Julie."

James placed his hand on Julie's as she lay there in the hospital bed.

"That just cannot be James ... I am still married to my husband and I need to give him another chance. Ask yourself James, what do you think the good Lord would do in this situation? You have said the same thing yourself from the pulpit James, you know that. You have said the same yourself, James, that this is the litmus test of our faith in any situation!"

"Yes but ..."

Michael walked in.

"Julie ... how are you my darling? Hello James, thank you for coming here to comfort Julie, I couldn't get here any sooner. Julie are you okay, are you in any pain?"

"I was but I have been heavily sedated, so it doesn't feel so bad now. I should have been more careful Michael."

Pastor James decided to leave Julie and Michael alone.

"I best be going now Julie, but you let me know if there is anything you need, okay."

"Okay thank you for coming James."

"Goodbye Michael."

"Goodbye James, thank you."

Pastor James left.

Julie and Michael just looked at each other for half a minute, both contemplating where to go from here – what to say next.

"Michael – I want you to know that I do understand, okay. I know I have not been there for you the way you wanted me to. I want you to know that I can forgive you Michael, but only if you promise me that you will never do anything like this again."

"Julie ... I will be the best husband in the world if you give me a chance to be. I will always be faithful to you."

Michael leaned forward to hug his wife as she lay in the bed. Just at that moment CXN introduced another well-known guest speaker.

Chapter 11

At the CXN studio a prominent and well respected New York social critic had been invited to telephone in to give his interpretation of the day's events.

"Okay we now have online our very well-known social commentator from radio 2NY here in New York Mr. Zach Ferodo - good morning to you Zach."

"Good morning Barbara, Tom and Alex well what a very special day this is, I have to state the obvious that we have never see anything like this before, but I think this is really exciting, I really do. I suppose I wouldn't be so upbeat about it had they started to blow the place apart but, hey, it seems we have some very friendly visitors here today."

"Yes and a lot of people out in the street have expressed the same, Zach and I am sure that they will be very pleased to hear you say the same because you are such a prominent feature here in New York City on the morning radio and you are very well respected right throughout the United States and indeed other parts of the world too for your views on just about everything – well on everything."

"Thank you, Barbara, yes I do my best."

"Zach just on that point I hope you don't mind if I digress just a little before we move on to the current situation, I listened intently to your commentary this morning about the latest shooting tragedy where eleven school students were gunned down by a disenchanted teacher last week in Georgia ... ah ... a teacher who had been fired by the school committee and I have got to say that within this entire debate about guns, you hit the nail right on the head."

"Well I hope so Alex, that is certainly how I see it, you know, so many Americans want to possess their guns, they know that there is going to be a mass shooting somewhere in the not too distant future but it's a bit like a lottery to them –

they know that in all probability it is going to be somebody else's child that is shot and killed – and they are right about that. The people who suffer and who do change their mind on the gun question, are the parents of the children who are shot and killed – they invariably then speak out calling for greater control and are left to get on with their shattered lives somehow, but the rest of the population and the gun lobby in particular, as you see, they still advocate that they deserve the right to bear arms. Which really is such a very callous disposition in my view. Some of them have even said that the children should be allowed to carry guns for the own self-defense. I mean, what would they regard as the lower age limit on that? Can you imagine all of our children aged over ten years turning up to school each day bearing a gun? I mean, really, some of those people are just plain stupid."

"Hmm ... yes thank you Alex for raising that issue as I was unaware of Zach's commentary on that this morning and I must say that does put a different perspective on the whole debate for me too. But one thing I did hear from you Zach just a couple of days ago when I was driving to work, which was quite timely given events here today, was Zach's commentary about the need for us to establish a human colony on Mars. Zach you must have known something was about to happen!"

"No Barbara I cannot lay claim to prior knowledge but I feel I was expressing the feelings of many of our eminent scientists on this because let's face it, the way we are going we might need a colony on Mars to survive. Now that NASA has seemingly detected flowing water on Mars it would be appropriate to establish a colony that has proximity to that water resource because such a colony would need to be totally self-sufficient. It would need to extract water for the purpose of growing crops such as vegetables, fruit and some grain crops, for human consumption and for animal husbandry too. Obviously we would send droids and robots there first to do some of the basic setup work, the domes and the infrastructure for water extraction, perhaps also some mining equipment for mineral extraction etcetera but it is something that we must undertake as an imperative."

"We have seen international cooperation on a number of fronts already to establish complex or expensive infrastructures, such as the International Space Station and the CERN Hadron Collider and to establish a base on Mars would require a similar joint effort and, you know, these things can bring nations closer together, so to involve the USA, the European nations, Russia, China, Canada and so on would make this project viable but also may go some way toward ameliorating our international relations even further."

"Sorry to interrupt, Zach, but I haven't heard that word before."

"To ameliorate simply means to make things better. There is no doubt that relations between the USA and the former Soviet Union improved immensely with the joint effort required for the space station. But we would also see some very wealthy individuals throw some resources at this too, the same way that they are contemplating taking people into space."

"Okay Zach that really is very interesting now Zach, give us some insights into what we are seeing here today. I am sure the whole of America wants to hear Zach Ferodo on this."

"Okay thank you Barbara, let me start by putting a type of biblical spin on this. Obviously you have heard from a number of religious people already this morning and you still have someone from the Vatican on the way as I believe and I am intrigued by what the speakers have had to say but not surprised. I always find some of those people intriguing because I can't always fathom how they come to believe what they put out there. It is as if God did not give some of them a brain."

"To hear the people from the Jehovah's Witnesses, then the Bible Discernment Ministry and then the Assembly of God people it does not surprise me at all that they were among the first three groups to call in. You see they all believe fervently that their own belief system is inerrant and that everybody else is errant, or wrong, so they would be quick to place some kind of a spin on this event that is in accordance with what they believe, and in some cases, as you saw, it came down to a grab for cash. Which is not surprising because for some of those people the only God they now have is money. They may have been good Christian people but many of them have been corrupted by money and everybody knows it."

"But my Biblical spin on this event is this. Consider the book of Genesis and the account of creation therein, well years ago a friend of mine told me that his interpretation was that the planet we live on is the Garden of Eden. I found that to be quite a plausible explanation actually, that God had given us this planet Earth as our Garden of Eden. Then about eighteen years ago my friend told me of something really astonishing. I think it was in 1997 when NASA decided to point the Hubble Telescope into deep space just to find out what was out there, even the most eminent scientists in the world could not believe what they discovered with the Hubble."

"Now most people would have no idea about this but the Hubble had to orbit the Earth about one hundred and sixty times and take a snapshot though this very tiny hole in the sky, where there were not too many stars or galaxies in the way to block one's view, with each orbit, just to compile a photograph of what was out there and the resultant photograph showed about three thousand galaxies. At least at that time NASA thought the number was about three thousand galaxies. But many years later - perhaps in 2004 - NASA enhanced the cameras on the Hubble and did the same again in the same place and the astronomers realized that there were actually about ten thousand galaxies within that tiny hole in space."

"Then I believe they did the same a few years later and discovered even more galaxies and they got an identical result from the southern hemisphere too. So I put it to my friend that if God did create the universe, why would he create so many billions of galaxies? Do you think that God created those galaxies so that we could look at them through the Hubble Telescope? No! God created those galaxies so that we can find a way to colonize the universe, so perhaps the universe is our Garden of Eden."

"Hey I sure hope you are right about that Zach - that would be amazing to think that we humans could someday, somehow conquer the universe."

"No Alex, I said to colonize not to conquer, we have done our share of conquering. But just think about it his way, if we were stuck here on planet Earth forever and unable to leave this place, given that it is eventually going to be swallowed up by the sun when the sun becomes a red giant, wouldn't it be such total folly for an almighty deity that we refer to as God and whom Muslim people refer to as Allah, to create all of those billions of galaxies without giving us sufficient intelligence to work out how to get there."

"And who knows, if we do survive long enough to start our sojourn into the cosmos, where will the technology take us to in say ten thousand years from now or in five billion years from now. By then we could be travelling through wormholes to the other side of the known universe in just a few seconds or even into parallel universes. I have heard Dr. Einstein and Dr. Michio Kaku and others refer to the possibility of there being a bubble bath of universes. That, by the way, is how it was put in the film 'Stargate' with Kurt Russell and James Spader – that the other planet was on the other side of the known universe and it didn't take them very long to get there either – just a few seconds in fact. So I fervently believe that now, that we are going to colonize the cosmos and there will never be too few stars and planets to keep us going. It seems that our friends are already quite some way down that road now, doesn't it?"

"It certainly does, now Zach apart from the cosmos aspects what can you say to our viewers that might be feeling somewhat bewildered by today's events, especially people who do believe in God and people who believe in Jesus in particular."

"Well Tim I thought the Archbishop of Canterbury was very prudent in advising people to just hold out for more information on this because we can't simply throw our religious beliefs out the window as soon as a spaceship turns up from another planet. I say that because as a believer in God myself I think he is working something out for us on this, okay. So everybody just keep calm and stay cool. And let's all hope for a good outcome from all of this."

"But Zach why now, why do you think these aliens would come here in this very overt way now?"

"Barbara, we live in troubled times as everybody knows. There are three significant and critical problems that we need to deal with now, so the aliens might have come here to assist us or to give us some guidance, considering that they may have survived considerably longer, it would seem, than we have. Those three things are the terrorism that now beleaguers our world, climate change that could completely destroy our world within our own lifetime and the appallingly anomalous distribution of wealth in our world today and the all of the problems that are concomitant with that. Why do we preside over a situation where so many millions of children are starving?"

"On the issue of terrorism that we see in the world today, there is no guarantee that things are going to work out the way we would all like them too. The radicals might continue to recruit ever-increasing numbers of young impressionable fighters who are prepared to sacrifice their own lives in pursuit of some misguided cause, such as eternity in paradise with twenty four virgins or seventy two virgins – I am unsure which is purportedly correct but I have heard both versions. Which is quite a worry when you think that these men obviously believe that the entire purpose of the life of the virgins is for them to have sex with, when they make it to paradise. I mean, what on earth are they thinking about those virgin women whose sole purpose in existence is to be there for those so-called martyrs to enjoy some sex? They obviously have a very poor view of those women, which seems to accord with the way that large sectors of Islamic men do think of women in the world today. As you know women are oppressed in many Islamic countries and the worst of them, ISIL and the Taliban, forbid women to be educated or to do so many normal day to day things, like drive a motor car or even to listen to popular music or watch television."

"The young fighters who are recruited are brainwashed into believing that they have to murder other people to make it to paradise. If this ISIL phenomenon continues to take hold it could give rise to the worst war in human history. So perhaps we humans are in need of some urgent assistance now and on this we just might be at the crossroads soon. Can you imagine what ISIL terrorists would do with nuclear weapons should they procure them? It seems to me that such an acquisition is definitely on their agenda. That could be the Armageddon referred to in the book of the Apocalypse. God help us if that should ever happen."

"On the question of climate change, things could be a lot worse than even the scientists believe. Okay so we have made some inroads into attenuating the hole in the ozone layer which seems to be on the decline but even so, the planet is heating up and presently virtually all glaciers in the world are retreating. You know we might reach a critical point in our lifetime where the North Pole melts away completely and Antarctica begins its big meltdown too. I have heard estimates that if the ice in Antarctica melts away the levels of the world's oceans will rise by about fifty feet, so all coastal cities would be under the ocean. In the States that would obviously include New York, large sections of San Francisco and Los Angeles and New Orleans and internationally cities like London, Paris Tokyo, Amsterdam, Dublin, Florence, Athens, Sydney, Melbourne, Auckland, Christchurch - in fact dozens of major cities would be completely drowned away because so many people live so close to the coastlines. Even cities well inland that are located on rivers would be flooded, such as Rotterdam in The Netherlands."

"And we see the utter devastation caused by hurricanes in our east-coast communities almost every year."

"Yes Tom and that critical point could come with just a one or two degree rise in the world's temperatures. Consider the destruction to coral reefs and the effect that will have on the environment. It was not that long ago that we saw a massive decline in the world's population of frogs, as the President mentioned and even today, they have still not recuperated to prior levels. We have seen similar problem with bees in recent times and we really do not know if climate change is a partial cause of these things. Okay we have identified a problem with a mite on bees but perhaps the mite thrives in warmer temperatures. Consider if a small increase in temperatures causes some plants or trees to die off. We have no idea of what type of domino effect that would cause on other forms of vegetation and insect life. We all know that we wouldn't be here without insects to pollinate flowers and trees. So the consequences could be catastrophic."

"And, Zach, on the distribution of the world's wealth?"

"How many more decades are going to pass, Barbara, before the governments of the world have sufficient gumption to tackle the pervasive taxation avoidance by our wealthiest people that denies so many governments of the resources to assist people in the world's poorest countries. We have seen famine take hold in Africa and South America and millions of people starve to death while people in western societies waste fortunes of precious money on cigarettes, alcohol, gambling, drugs, building their mansions, fast cars, guns and all of the other luxury items that we believe we need to live. Your average citizen will build a bigger and better house with more mod cons than settle for something a little more modest and financially support children through World Vision or the Catholic Missions. In affluent societies people want a more expensive motor car, they want to progress to the boat or the caravan or the home cinema or to investment properties without giving a small part of their wealth to alleviating some suffering in the world. Some of our religious leaders are among the worst examples of this accumulation of wealth and we have seen so many of them make themselves extremely wealthy by preaching the Gospel, as some of you previous guests have alluded to."

"Have we got our priorities right? No, we have not! So until we do something quite drastic about that, there will always be some angst against western culture from the poorer nations and on that I need to reiterate that it is some of the wealthiest people in the world today, the shareholders of corporations like Apple and Google and our largest mining companies that are the main offenders when it comes to taxation avoidance."

"So you think they might have come here to help us with some of these issues Zach?"

"That is certainly my take on the events this morning, yes and I do believe we need help right now to avert some serious calamity."

"Zach one thing I picked up on there was that you said these aliens may have survived longer than we have, well, wouldn't it be obvious that they have?"

"I will reserve judgement on that Tom because, when you look at the history of the human race since civilization commenced in Mesopotamia about nine thousand years ago, we have been beating hell out of each other and that may have been a major impediment to our progress. When you look at how the world has advanced in the very short time since the inception of, say, the dynamo, which can generate electricity from movement or vice versa by utilizing magnetism, how much sooner would we have become the civilized people that we are today if the Egyptians had developed electric power and we did not have such a propensity for conflict. So perhaps an alien civilization based on cooperation and without major conflict could achieve what we have in the last nine thousand years in, say, two thousand years. So perhaps they have developed more quickly even if they haven't survived longer than the human race. After all we homo-sapiens have been here for a couple of hundred thousand years now."

"Zach Ferodo thank you for sharing with us this morning and, Zach, please don't go away because we might ask you some more shortly because I believe we will have a representative from the Vatican on-line very soon.

You are watching CXN and our very special live telecast of this most extraordinary event here in New York City – something we have never seen the likes of before and now we do have a senior member of the Vatican on-line and it is a very good morning to the most reverend Cardinal James Gilroy, who is originally from the United States, in fact originally from Santa Fe in California. Good morning Cardinal Gilroy."

"Good morning to you Barbara Foster and to your companions Mr. Tom Lowry and Mr. Alex Dwyer."

"Thank you, Your Grace, no doubt the Vatican would have been keenly observing this unfolding situation here this morning in New York City but may I begin by asking if you managed to observe any of the preceding commentary here this morning from religious leaders? We have heard from a number of leaders from all over the world though especially from here in the United States and it is already clear to see why a lot of people are so very confused when it comes to religious beliefs. The common feeling that must prevail among so many people out there is 'who am I supposed to believe'? But perhaps more importantly what is the Catholic Church's take on this most extraordinary event?"

"Well firstly I must concur whole heartedly with the views expressed by the Archbishop of Canterbury on this that patience is a virtue and we must wait to learn more of these people and from these people who are so many years advanced on us in terms of their technology. They have found a way of traversing space or space-time as we now refer to it and it is very re-assuring that their initial intent seems to be one of peace. They are obviously highly intelligent and very civilized people, which is very encouraging for us, to know that life can prosper to the point where it is possible to traverse our own galaxy and quite possibly even beyond that."

"I believe it is absolutely imperative for me to state that it is important to maintain our faith in God in times like this for He will provide answers. If aliens are for real - and it seems that the present situation that is unfolding there in New York City indicates that they are - then it must be part of God's plan for us. We must always remain cognizant that as much as we might believe that we know the mind of God or the will of God, we do not come even close to knowing God - neither his mind nor his will, except to say that God is eternally good."

174

"Ah ... yes we did have a similar kind of assurance from the Archbishop of Canterbury, your Grace, who encouraged people all over the world to ... ah ... try to keep an open mind about this and to not start jumping to too many conclusions about the religious implications at this point of time. It seems that perhaps you, yourself, would affirm that position now of the Bishop of Canterbury."

"Yes I do, I believe he cautioned people against being too worried about this, but I would also like to remind people of a very important verse from the letter of Saint Paul to the Romans and this is verse twenty eight from chapter eight, where Saint Paul wrote "We know that in all things God works together for goodness with those who love him" and from this we find hope and faith that whatever happens in our world or in our lives, for those who do respect and believe in God or, even in the broader sense, all good people, God will always draw something good from whatever happens to us."

"So you would expect, Your Grace, that God will educe some type of good works from this cataclysmic event? Do you have any idea how he might do that, given that this event here today just might signal the termination of all hitherto existing religious belief systems?"

"I would ask everybody to think of God in terms of him being an almighty deity who created the universe in which we live and in which our visitors here today also live and given what we know of the universe now – its vastness and its complexity – to think of God as being of infinite intelligence and of infinite power, which he must be in order to have created the universe, also of infinite knowledge and infinite wisdom, but most importantly of infinite love and of infinite mercy. So the God that I have come to know right throughout my lifetime is a God who will do positive things for us as a humanity, as a human race made in his image. He is not about to leave us stranded and disillusioned and totally bewildered by this advent of alien life. No! I am sure that this is a part of his greater plan for us and that his love for us will shine though here somehow."

"Now I know what everybody is thinking, where does this put Jesus and what does the Catholic Church believe in that respect. Well I have to let you know that very soon after these events started to unfold his holiness Pope Francis II did call for an emergency on-line conference of all Catholic Cardinals and Archbishops who were available, which was quite a large number of people as you could imagine. Some were not available, but we did have a forum of more than one hundred to discuss this with the Pontiff who actually was giving guidance on this rather than receiving it. Pope Francis really was quite an extraordinary man. The word from our Pontiff was to maintain our faith in God and to extend our love to these visitors, whoever they are and wherever they come from."

"Huh ... extend our love?"

"Yes Barbara, Pope Francis made special reference to the encounter of Jesus with the rich young man and we are aware of the discussions you had earlier with Professor Jones who did raise this very important encounter of Jesus with the rich young man. What our Pontiff asked us to remember above all, is what is recorded in the gospel about the initial response of Jesus to the question put to him by the rich young man which was, of course, 'Lord what must I do to enter the kingdom of Heaven?'"

"And the initial answer the Lord gave to him was to follow the Ten Commandments!"

"Well yes, Barbara, that was the initial answer from our Lord but I am actually referring to what is recorded in the gospel, as the initial response from Jesus."

"And that was?"

"That was that he looked at the rich young man and he loved him."

"Now that – is Jesus Christ! That is the response from the Son of God, to a young man who was trying to find his way through life, a very good young man who was searching for total fulfilment in his life and, despite being very good and very charitable in giving a lot of assistance to the poor, knew there was more in life than what, even he, had.

"So we believe that our response to these people who are probably very good people too, must be one of love. This is the message from our Pontiff, Pope Francis that we must be prepared to love everybody – even if they do come from outer space."

Everybody chuckled.

"But where does this put Jesus? We heard one young man state that Jesus was a fraudster and quite a few people would be thinking the same thing. If there are aliens out there on other planets in other galaxies where does that put Jesus?"

"Perhaps Jesus did choose us to take his Gospel of love to the universe. I am very keen to hear what the President has to say on that when he addresses the people again, that is whether or not these visitors can shed any light for us on the life of Jesus Christ. After all, a lot of people do believe that aliens have been visiting the Earth for many thousands of years – perhaps even pre-dating the lifetime of Jesus Christ."

"Yes well hopefully these aliens are not going to say anything that will make a total mockery of our religious beliefs as that young man expressed earlier, but Your Grace, are you able to shed some Catholic light on what we have heard hear this morning from the other preachers of religion. We heard for example, from the Jehovah's Witnesses who would have us believe that this is the Lord himself who has been in the upper air since about the year 1914, we have heard from the Scientologists who have stated that they believe these visitors are the purest of thetans and that we are all, in fact, thetans too and we have heard from a number of ministers from the Assembly of God who are encouraging people to donate ten per cent of everything they own in order to be saved. What do you think about all of that?"

"Barbara, my advice to everybody would be to take it all with a grain of salt, be skeptical even cynical about such things because there are too many people out there who purport to know the mind of God and often they are people who read their Bible and come to a false realization that they have been enlightened by God and that they know some new truth, or they have been misguided by somebody else. The Jehovah's Witnesses, the Mormons and the Scientologists are classical examples of that, where one person came to such a realization and then set about spruiking that belief and credulous people followed. Charles Taze Russell initiated the Jehovah's Witnesses and within conventional Christian circles they are considered to have cultist traits and they mislead people with false doctrine and a part of that is their rejection of other religious belief systems and of fellow Christians."

"But for all their warts and faults the Catholic Church still regards them as good Christian people. That is the most cogent way I can express that. Essentially, they are Christian people with a close relationship with God, even if they do denounce everybody else. We don't hold that against them because we understand how they have been misled the Catholic Church needs to be the guiding light that will bring people closer together, despite their lack of understanding of the nature of God."

"Now on the matter of criticism levelled toward the Catholic Church by Protestants – and there is certainly no paucity of this – I must state that the Catholic Church does not engage in reprisal against other religions, be they Christian, Muslim or any others. We are fully aware of the incessant outpourings from some sections of Protestant churches against the Catholic Church as we have teams of eminent theologians who keep abreast of such things, but there will never be any form of reprisal initiated against naysayers. The Catholic Church must be seen as the instigator of inclusivism and ecumenism, without bickering on pedantic details of doctrine. We refer to such pedantic doctrinal bickering as frivolous fundamentalist folly – most of which emanates from Protestants in the United States, of course."

"But as we clearly see from all Christian churches and our Islamic brothers too, some people stray from the path – they usually allow an ulterior consideration to cloud their understanding of what is required of them – be that money, power, violence, politics, sex or ego. Within the Catholic priesthood we have never had a problem with our priests straying for reasons pertaining to money or power or politics, but we have had the problem of the sexual abuse of children and we are confident that we have been able to extirpate those who have offended or those who might offend. We have had to acknowledge now that our requirement of celibacy for our priesthood has been a significant factor in that. Many of my fellow Cardinals - and indeed I myself - are encouraging Pope Francis to expunge that requirement now and we believe that we do have the right pontiff to achieve that, in the not too distant future."

"Now returning to your question, Barbara, I must state that some sections of American Protestantism have a proclivity or tendency to be extremely dogmatic and to theologically banish all people who are not overtly Christian. Some of those believe that Muslim people will not be saved because the Protestants I refer to believe that Muslim people worship a false God."

"They believe this because in the book of Sura the Prophet Mohammed wrote that people who believe in the Trinity or believe that Jesus was or is the Son of God or that Jesus is God, are blasphemers. It is because Muslim people espouse their belief that the name of God is Allah - whom they would equate with the Father within the Trinity - that conservative, traditional, dogmatic Christians believe that Muslim people worship a false God. Such Protestants don't see the total folly of their misguided attitude toward Muslim people."

"Why do they believe that an almighty deity they know as God, who created the universe and everything within it, would damn people for eternity because they refer to him as Allah rather than God? The answer to that comes back to what the psychologist had to say about spite or malice and, peculiarly, that many such Christians do seem to feel better about themselves by believing that hundreds of millions of other people in the world – Muslim people or Hindu people or Buddhist people – are going to be damned. As Dr. Bates said, that disposition smacks of being totally devoid of Christian love."

"As the sociologist Professor Jones pointed out, more than ninety-five per cent of the human race who do maintain or subscribe to a religious belief system, be it Islam, Christianity, Hinduism or Buddhism, will maintain the belief into which they were born and into which they were socialized from birth."

"Why do fundamentalist Christians or Muslims believe that the almighty God or Allah would banish all believers in the other creed for eternity, when the religious belief of such an enormous portion of the human population is pre-determined by the geographic and historical location assigned to them at birth and in which they have no choice?"

"The Catholic Church does not believe that Muslim people will be banished in that way, in fact the official disposition of the Catholic Church is that Muslim people and Christian people all worship the same God, regardless of whether or not one believes in the Trinity and regardless of what name people give to God. This was very clearly espoused through the official Catholic Church proclamation the 'Nostra Aetate' in October 1965."

"The Catholic Church promulgated the doctrine of Nostra Aetate in October 1965 following the conclusion of the Second Vatican Council instigated by its, then, recently deceased Pontiff John the Twenty Third. In the Nostra Aetate the Church made it patently clear that it embraced Islam and all Muslim people as belonging to the same church of God on earth – despite some fundamental differences in doctrine pertaining to whether Jesus is God.

"Does that actually mean that the Catholic Church believes that Muslim people are destined for heaven?"

"Yes of course it does, of course they are, providing they live their lives as good people."

"And the same for Hindu and Buddhist people?"

"The same for all people - we acknowledge Jesus as our Lord in being Christ-like. We have come to realize the folly of trying to quantify the mind of God except to think of him as being all powerful and merciful and loving."

"But returning to where I was a moment ago, Catholics refer to the Father within the Trinity as Yahweh – that is his name. As a slight digression here, perhaps I ought to point out for people who do not realize this, but this is the name that Charles Russell who founded the Jehovah's Witnesses altered into 'Jehovah'. He simply decided for himself that the Catholics had misinterpreted the name of the Father and contrived his own version of God's name, even though he was totally uneducated in either Hebrew or theology. I mention that to emphasize further that it really does not matter what name you confer upon God the Father or whether you believe in the Trinity or don't believe it – after all the concept of the Trinity has befuddled people since its inception, since it was

181

first acknowledged as the meaning of the Gospel, in the first century A.D."

"The concept has befuddled people because Jesus did say some things that can be taken either way. He said for example that 'the Father is greater than I am' but he also said, 'the Father has no power over me'. So how could God the Father who is greater than Jesus, himself, have no power over Jesus if Jesus was simply a man and a prophet?"

"Perhaps what really swayed the early church was another profound proclamation by Jesus, when he said "I am in the Father and the Father is in me' and also to his reference to the helper, the Holy Spirit of God coming to the disciples after his own ascension into Heaven and he spoke of the Holy Spirit of God as being an equal entity with himself, not as an angel nor a prophet."

"Furthermore he referred to himself as 'the Son of Man' which has been taken to mean God the Son of Man and his referring to himself as 'I am who am' which the Jews of the day regarded as a claim to deity. When Jesus forgave sins, the Jews said it very clearly – 'who but God can forgive sins' and when they challenged him on this he said 'which of these is easier to forgive sins or to say pick up they bed and walk' so he commanded the lame man to walk."

"So we know that Jesus said a lot of things to infer that he and the Father were one, but the Catholic Church does understand that still some people who read their Bible and believe they have become enlightened by God, will have difficulty understanding the concept of the Trinity. We do not think less of them for this."

"So the God we know and love who created all things would not - I say would not - damn people to hell for eternity depending on what they call him by name or whether or not they believe in God as a single deity as Muslim people do, or whether they believe in the Trinity, as most Christians do. In fact some Christian denominations, such as the Jehovah's Witnesses, also do not believe in the Trinity. They too, believe that Jesus was a prophet but not God. And yes, as I have stated, we do regard the Jehovah's Witnesses as Christians even though they, themselves, believe that they are the only Christians and that everybody else belongs to Satan's empire."

"Consider this! In 1864 a very famous American, William Penn, was required to preside over the trial of Margaret Mattson, the witch of Ridley Creek. William Penn presiding as the judge ruled that there was no law within the province that made it unlawful for a person to practice witchcraft and so dismissed the case. He was later confronted by a group of people who were bent on burning the woman at the stake. His response to them is etched and ensconced within the American psyche and most of us know what that was. 'If any person thinks they can ride a broomstick, let them'.

"This had a profound impact on everybody and on the development of the United States of America Constitution and today we believe the same. If people want to believe that they are the only people who are going to be saved by almighty God, let them. Their belief does not, cannot and never will have any bearing on the will of God. But as your psychologist has pointed out, the true motivation for such beliefs needs to be further analyzed by that profession with research into the psychology of dogmatism."

"You have made reference there, in passing, to people who read their Bible and believe they have been enlightened by God, well, do you think that is also quite a profound aspect within the history of Christianity?"

"It would be a gross understatement to say 'yes' to that Tom and it seems to be a trend here in the United States of America more than anywhere else. If you delve into the history of Protestant churches such as the Methodist, Congregational and Presbyterian churches you can find their

183

origins attributable to some rather pedantic differences of doctrine that emanates from European origins. So at the time of the re-unification of the Methodist, Presbyterian and Congregational churches in both Canada and Australia, for example, it was acknowledged that they had so much in common and so few differences in their essential doctrine that it made such great sense to unite. And thank God they have! People need to do more to set aside their pedantic differences in doctrine to focus more on the essence of the Gospel, the immense and infinite love of God for everybody and our love for neighbor as self."

"But here in the States in more recent times we have witnessed the advent of American Protestantism going down the road of Pentecostalism and other evangelical movements that may not be Pentecostal but have similar levels of enthusiasm and even hype. That is so wonderful that they become so engrossed in their relationship with the Lord that they display such fervor and zeal for their relationship with God and I also subscribe to the comments by Professor Jones that this is what the Lord was seeking from the rich young man."

"Which probably tells us in the Catholic Church that we fall short in that respect because we rely so much on the Mass and the seven Sacraments to cater for our spiritual needs. Hence, when a Catholic person does develop such a profound love of the Lord from that commitment, they find our church is rather staid and they don't really have anywhere to go for community with similar enthusiastic people unless they become part of the Charismatic movement. Unfortunately, this movement has inherited the fallacy of the gift of tongues from American Pentecostals and, to a far lesser extent, some of the spurious dogmatism too. At least within the Catholic Church the priest and other clergy can mitigate some of that dogmatism, whereas many Protestants preachers do tend to thrive on it."

"I was very keenly listening to your earlier guests the sociologist and the psychologist and their references to what I would generally refer to as people's motives in the development of religious doctrine. There is quite some truth in what they had to say about the money motives and the bigotry – the malice or spite for anybody who is different - which is a very unfortunate by-product of those movements and one that is totally inappropriate."

"And is that because, as Professor Jones said, they make more money that way?"

"Well that is a matter for the good Lord himself to judge, but it does seem to be quite a factor in everything they do. If you watch the televangelists on television in the early hours of the morning, it seems that almost everything that some of them do always comes back to money. This is not to denigrate those that are genuinely raising funds for good works, except there seems to be a lack of true accountability for the use of the funds, but in the past some have been quite blatant and very brazen too, in their pursuit of money and have seemingly taken very good care of themselves, financially, and many people around them too – family, relatives and their coterie of cohorts of various kinds."

"So I am not going to pull any punches here! One does not have to be judgemental to assert that, historically speaking, many of our prominent televangelists have literally thrown Almighty God out the window for love of money. They set out following the Lord, as he implored of the rich young man to 'come and follow me'. Then they invoked the spurious doctrine of tithings to achieve financial security, but the love of money takes hold of so many of them, who then promulgated what we know as 'prosperity doctrine'. Many years ago I observed Benny Hinn assert to his flock that 'God wants you to be wealthy - and how can I preach this to you if I, myself, am poor?' He seemed to expediently overlook that

Jesus was born in a manger and rode into Jerusalem on a donkey and was, therefore, the epitome of humility and of poverty. In fact, there is no reference in the gospel to Jesus owning anything. I was also flabbergasted about the same time to observe Gloria Copeland exclaim 'you think the Lord wants to wrench your hand open to get your tithings' followed by her husband, Kenneth, so arrogantly and condescendingly stand before the congregation twiddling his thumbs and stating 'now you non-tithers' - as if to question whether they would be welcomed into the kingdom of heaven. So this exaction of tithings had become blatant and flagrant theft in my opinion and still is today."

"Yes, I think a lot of people will agree with you on that one Professor Jones."

"In fact I believe this is the very reason why, back in the year 2007, United States Senator Chuck Grassley of Iowa initiated the Senate inquiry into such activities. It is also the reason that Ole Anthony of the Trinity Foundation has been so scathingly critical of televangelists usurping substantial amounts of money from their church's funds. Fortunately the Assembly of God now has the committee to enforce some accountability on evangelists and as a result we have witnessed the relative demise of some of the worst offenders but within the hegemony of the church there would, nevertheless, be a presiding belief that everybody who does God's work as a preacher needs to be taken good care of financially."

"In fact, that same notion comes through from the findings of the Senate inquiry – that even though the televangelists who were investigated had annual personal incomes of millions of dollars, the committee found that none of those who cooperated had a case to answer."

"But it does seem to be, an unfortunate truth, that the most successful televangelists are the most dogmatic ones."

"I have been quite astonished to witness people within the congregation of some of those who denigrate Muslim people, for example, displaying signs not only of acceptance of doctrine being promulgated, but definite signs of gleeful concurrence – such as smiling, nodding of the head, clapping of the hands and utterances of endorsement."

"One example of that was a very well-known televangelist who was on stage saying things like 'you cannot be saved by the Prophet Mohammed, you cannot be saved by re-incarnation, you cannot be saved by going to church every Sunday, you cannot be saved by receiving the sacraments of the Catholic Church'. The people in the congregation were shaking their head saying 'no, no, no' with a frown on their faces whenever he said that 'you cannot be saved by' those various beliefs. He then went on to say 'you can only be saved by repenting of your sins, by renouncing Satan and all his works, by being born again, by accepting the Lord Jesus Christ as your personal Lord and savior and by being baptized in the Holy Spirit - and evidence of this is that you pray in tongues'. Everybody was nodding their approval and saying 'yes, yes, yes' and smiling."

"So a social scientist or researcher, such as a psychologist or a sociologist, might regard those responses as being very reliable indicators of the extent to which spite towards non-Christians is a substantial aspect of their motivation."

"But to return to the point, yes there is a very strong proclivity within Protestant circles for money to be the largest impediment to sanctity and within Islam, it is the politics."

"Our Muslim brothers would do well to heed the advice from the late Pope John Paul II who advised them not to confuse their politics and their religion. The modern-day terrorist is a person who was raised into Islam but became politically aggrieved – for whatever reason – and failed to distinguish the true reason for their grievance. Their exhortations to Islam due to their political grievances, whatever they may be, are essentially a case of misplaced conflict. As your psychologist said 'hypocrisy abrogates belief' so once they resort to violence, they virtually repeal any claim they have to be a Muslim person. They seem to be envious of western lifestyle but the inequalities within their own nation are typically quite profound because of the way that dictators and the military establishment usurp such massive amounts of their nation's wealth, usually for the purpose of perpetuating power. North Korea epitomizes that fact today more than any other nation, but autocrats such as Saddam Hussein, Muammar Gaddafi, the Marcos couple in the Philippines and the Suharto and Sukarno families in Indonesia are classic examples of that too."

"And Your Grace you said that within American Protestantism it is money that might be, what, an obstacle to faith?"

"Yes Barbara, in respect of the Assembly of God we do have a standard matter of jocularity within the Vatican that the Assembly of God's version of the Sermon on the Mount, has become the 'sermon on the amount'. That is, of course, the amount of money that believers need to give to their pastor in order to be 'saved', as they put it."

"Yes we did hear from Professor Jones on this earlier and he was quite cynical about this practice of virtually coercing substantial amounts of money from people."

"Well Tom it seems to be peculiarly American by origin although all nations where the Assembly of God is active are virtually doing the same thing but the televangelists are very strong on warning people about the power of Satan having an influence on their lives so perhaps they should spend more time pondering whether Satan has corrupted themselves with money. We in the Catholic Church don't bewilder or harass people with talk about Satan. We do believe there is no need to give so much money to your church and that every person has a personal responsibility to take care of their own personal financial security first, without going too far on that I might add and I would concur with your previous speaker Mr. Zach Ferodo on that too. Then once they have financial security they can help others but this concept of tithings is not consistent with Catholic teaching and smacks of usurpation and even psychological extortion."

"We believe that most Catholics give about ten to twenty dollars each week and that is enough. Some give more because they can and some give less because they have financial problems such as being unemployed or in trying to raise large numbers of children, as many Catholics do. So we don't suggest any set amounts for people to contribute, there is no duress within the Catholic Church on that and my advice to all Protestants everywhere is to follow the Catholic tradition and give according to your conscience. Saint Paul wrote exactly that in his second letter to the Corinthians, but it seems that Protestant evangelists ignore that out of expediency."

And your Grace what does the Catholic Church teach about this other phenomenon that we have heard about here of this gift of tongues? Does the Catholic Church teach that this gift is genuine or not?"

"No, the Catholic Church does not teach that this phenomenon is genuine and we believe that it is not genuine. The position of the Catholic Church, officially, is that this supposed gift is not genuine and is probably a contrivance – one that is explainable, historically speaking and in terms of its acceptance by large numbers of people since about one hundred years ago here in the United States, but it is not the gift of tongues that was bestowed upon the Apostles at the first Pentecost. The Apostles were able to speak with real languages – Greek, Hebrew, Arabic. In fact according to the

Acts of the Apostles when Saint Peter and the other Apostles were speaking to groups of people that included people from different nations they each heard the speaker in their own language – the Jews heard Hebrew and the Greeks heard Greek."

"Nor is it regarded by the Catholic Church as being genuinely a gift of the Holy Spirit of God. We are aware of the research that has been conducted into this by very reputable social scientists and we do keep abreast of such things. A very compelling example of that was the acknowledgement of the theory of evolution by Pope Pius the Twelfth in the year 1954, by way of Papal Encyclical. We had to acknowledge the scientific evidence and accept that the Book of Genesis was a metaphorical account of creation - that God put his spirit into man who had evolved from an ancestor that we shared with other primates."

"Some extremely reputable university researchers conducted comprehensive analyses of the sounds, syllables, phrases, accent and intonation of this phenomenon of glossolalia and concluded that this supposed gift of tongues is phonologically structured human utterance but only a façade of a language."

"I believe what initiated this research was a skit in a junior school in North Virginia where students were re-enacting the arrival of The Pilgrims at Plymouth in 1620 on the Mayflower and their initial interactions were with the indigenous Indian people. The students were told to just make up a language or pretend they were talking in the Indian language and in this group of students and teachers there were some Pentecostal Christians. One such student said to a Pentecostal teacher that it sounded like they were praying in tongues and another teacher who was a linguist specialist enquired as to what they meant. That teacher forwarded the video recording to the National Institute of Linguists for analyses by researchers conducting their PhD studies. Those researchers then sought out a group of Pentecostal Christians supposedly praying in tongues and made numerous recordings – sometimes quite covertly – and completed their theses that literally demonstrated there was no difference between what the junior school students did when they contrived a totally artificial language and what the Pentecostal Christians were doing."

"You've probably heard it said that within the scientific method you cannot use something to prove itself – so for example you cannot use the Bible to prove that it, itself, is inerrant. Well we regard this supposed gift of tongues as being self-fulfilling. People are cajoled into using glossolalia as evidence of being baptized in the Holy Spirit and when they do they are told that the glossolalia is evidence that they have been baptized in the Holy Spirit."

"Hypothetically you could induct newcomers into a sporting team by telling them they must first display this glossolalia and when they do you admit them to your team, so that is the simple analogy of the practice but it is also true."

"So those people are being misled?"

"Yes it is a fallacy and what is unfortunate about the practice is that the Assembly of God erroneously teaches that it is a prerequisite for salvation. It is a strange thing that a single idea can become such a vital aspect of a major religious movement that affects millions of people, as with this fallacy of this supposed gift of tongues and with Ron L. Hubbard's idea that we are all thetans who have been transplanted here onto this planet, but these ideas can catch on with gullible or even just credulous people and can become a religious movement. Other compelling examples of how such a process can operate would include the Heaven's Gate community who committed mass suicide in 1997 because of the Comet Hale-Bopp and the Jonestown mass suicide in Guyana in 1978. One man convinced the Heaven's Gate people that they had to end their lives in order to be taken away on a spaceship that was obscured behind the comet."

"But the Catholic Church does not discourage people from believing in things such as this supposed gift of tongues if they choose to. You see, the Catholic Church does not degenerate into any form of religious bickering now – it is counterproductive and always leads to enmity. Nor is there ever any duress imposed upon people now, we must be open minded, tolerant and flexible with understanding. The mind of God will always be far greater than we can possibly comprehend. Where the fundamentalist and dogmatic teachers of religion go wrong is in the way they denigrate others who either take part in the normal church life or who live the life of what we now refer to as the 'anonymous Christian', people who do live their lives the same way that Jesus did, with love and compassion for other people and I am very pleased to state that this probably includes the vast majority of the human race."

"And is this what Jesus meant when he said we must be born again?

"Yes, Barbara, that is what Jesus meant."

"The Pentecostals believe they are born again and other people are not."

"Again, Barbara, this idea probably emanated from one individual who interpreted the scripture erroneously, but it made sense to people of that ilk and that spurious interpretation became the basis of their entire religion. The total commitment they have made to living their lives closely to Jesus is not what he meant when he said we must be born again. This is another example of a self-fulfilling concept. They equated their experience with those words from Jesus and, unfortunately, this has given rise to profound bigotry against so many others – against people from all other religious persuasions including other Christians. And that doctrine is, in fact, errant."

"We in the Catholic Church contend that all good people will go to heaven because Jesus died for our sins and that intrinsic within the Great Commandment of Jesus Christ, is that all good people do in fact follow the Ten Commandments and in doing so they also love God. Jesus did say that his Great Commandment – to love God and to love your neighbor as yourself - was the meaning of the Ten Commandments and the teaching of the prophets."

"Of course the Ten Commandments were handed to Moses as a very prescriptive set of laws for people to observe to live life close to God in that time prior to Jesus, but Jesus gave us his commandment that subsumed the Ten Commandments and gave that law new meaning. I do concur also with your previous guest that in living a life of goodness that is in accordance with the Ten Commandments any person is virtually Christ like and worthy of being re-united with God."

"Thank you, your Grace Cardinal Gilroy, for providing us with this assurance from the Catholic Church here this morning. I am sure that a lot of people will be greatly relieved to hear what you had to say. We do realize that here in the States the Catholic Church does have a larger congregation than any other church. Now to all those people phoning in with your credit cards to give your ten per cent to save your soul – put that phone down now."

"Are we receiving ...? Yes, we do believe the President is quite possibly ready to address the people once again, very soon."

Chapter 12

Earlier when the President arrived back in the rooftop conference room the Zircon high priest Zora handed the President the second gift – a rather odd looking small metallic disc about the size of a large coin. The President bowed his thanks then placed the disc onto the small table that the aide had brought into the room, alongside the box.

Zora reached out and touched the device and the small box activated a visual display onto the white wall of the room. Within a few seconds there appeared a very well-defined image of the planet, Earth, as seen from outer space, perhaps from about one third of the distance to the moon. The President and his top aide Ralph Lee were standing side by side looking at the image.

"That's one very clear image of our Earth there Ralph."

"Yes sir, it is!"

"I must say I haven't seen it that clear before!"

"No nor I, sir!"

Then the image started to zoom in on the planet, getting closer and closer and closer.

"So they are focusing now on the Mediterranean, the middle east."

"Yes sir!"

"Is that Israel?"

"Yes sir, I would say it certainly is!"

"Looks like a very clear day there – no clouds about. What city is that? I don't believe I recognize that part of Israel, Ralph."

"Ah ... that would seem to be where the city of Jerusalem is located sir."

"Looks rather different to the Jerusalem that I know."

The video footage zooms in even closer, to a particular part of the city, an open area filled with people.

"Ralph, tell me who those people are dressed that way."

"Ah ... they look like they are in some type of military uniform, sir."

"What are they doing? Oh my God! Did you see that – they have that man against that pillar and they have started to whip him. What's that on his head?"

"Oh my God - sir!" Ralph points to the lower left corner of the screen. "The time and date, sir!"

The President looked to where his aide Ralph was pointing and in a subdued voice read the details from the corner of the screen.

"Ten twenty-one, a.m., April twenty fifth ... why the four zero's?"

"Oh my God! I don't believe it! This can't be!"

"Ralph, what is this?"

"Oh my God! It's the year zero, sir!"

"Ralph? You're not making any sense. What do you mean?"

Ralph let out a deep sigh then took a deep breath and tried to collect himself for what he was about to say.

"Ah ... it's the scourging at the pillar sir. They are not using whips sir, they are using cat 'o nine tails sir!"

"Ralph ... do you mean *the* scourging at *the* pillar? Are you telling me that we are looking at Jesus Christ?"

"Ah ... yes sir, we are ... but ... I don't believe it!"

"Oh my God, can this be for real? Look at all that blood. Tell me what I am seeing here, Ralph."

"I think this is the passion of Jesus Christ, sir!" said Ralph, his voice wavering and started to crumble with emotion.

"What! I'm losing it Ralph. How can this be?"

Ralph tried to compose himself by taking a deep swallow. He turned to look at the high priests, who bowed their heads. Then he turned back to his President.

"Sir, they come from a planet that is more than two thousand light years away. They have been able to capture this light that has not even reached their planet yet sir. To record this they would simply have to move toward Earth from their planet and monitor the events occurring in that part of Earth until they found the right day then move back toward their planet at light speed to obtain virtual still shots if they wanted to or, alternatively, they could move slightly faster or slower than light speed to make an adjustment for the time sir. Then it would simply be a matter of compilation of the imagery, sir."

"Yes, of course! My God! How many lashings has that been?"

"About twenty-six sir!"

"How many do they give him?"

"Thirty-nine sir!"

"My God look at that! Not only all over his back but over his buttocks too and now over the back of his legs. There's blood everywhere. How could anyone survive this?"

"It seems that he nearly didn't sir – which is why he fell shortly after they made him take up his cross. You may recall, sir, they got a man named Simon to assist him. This is totally in accordance with the injuries depicted on the Holy Shroud of Turin sir."

The President's press secretary Lynda Lightfoot who was standing behind Ralph started to dry reach, causing the President to look around sharply, but she quickly composed herself again.

"You realize Ralph that we are the first human beings to see this since it happened more than two thousand years ago."

"Ah ... yes sir – I feel very humbled right now, sir. I happen to be a practicing Catholic, sir. He is my Lord!"

The President looked at Ralph. That was one thing he did not know about his closest aide. Ralph had a totally distraught look on his face.

The Roman soldiers stopped their flogging and the body of Jesus hung there at the pillar limply and motionless for many minutes as blood gushed from his wounds. It seemed the soldiers had decided to allow his body to stop bleeding – for the blood to coagulate - before allowing anyone to go near him.

Then the footage jumped suddenly to a different scene – the nailing of Jesus to the cross. The President and his aide Ralph were taken aback by the sudden change - but they were in no doubt as to what they were seeing. The President and his aides went into a state of shock, with the feeling of blood swelling in their heads and tears forming in their eyes. Jesus was lying on the cross, which was on the ground, the Roman soldiers had stretched out his arms and were nailing both his wrists to the cross. Blood spurted as they drove the nails in to the flesh. Some of his Apostles were visible in the background, standing back about twenty yards from the cross, where two men were comforting a small woman dressed in a blue and white cape.

Then the soldiers drove a nail into Jesus' right foot and placed his right foot above his left foot to drive the nail through his left foot and into the wood of the cross.

The woman in the background clasped both her arms around her stomach and bowed her head with pain and with sorrow.

The Roman soldiers then commenced the process of lifting the cross into the upright position, requiring several of them to work together, until the cross fell into the hole in the ground where it would come to rest. The soldiers then secured the cross in the upright position with some wooden stays, which they hammered into the ground around the foot of the cross. Once they had completed this task, all of them, but one, stood back several yards from the cross, looked up at Jesus and started to pat each other on the shoulders, as if to mutually acknowledge a job well done. The footage stayed with this scene for several minutes, showing many people in the background comforting each other, some weeping quite openly, but others in the foreground seemingly jeering at Jesus as he hung on the cross.

"My God Ralph, we have just witnessed the crucifixion of Jesus Christ. It was just as I had always imagined it to be. Ralph!"

Ralph was just staring at the images on the wall and shaking his head from side to side with tears rolling down his cheeks. At the sight of this – the crucifixion of his Lord, Jesus, he was completely mesmerized.

Then, suddenly, the footage jumped again, to a different scene. All of the people had disappeared. There was a tranquil type of garden setting with nobody present, just some trees, some bushes, some shrubs and a lot of colorful flowers in bloom. There were red flowers, yellow flowers, white flowers, pink flowers, orange flowers, green flowers and even some blue flowers.

The President and his aides just stood there watching, waiting for something to happen.

"Ralph, tell me what this is."

"Ah ... I have no idea sir."

Everybody was silent. The President turned and looked over his shoulder at the alien leader, who merely gave a slight bow of his head, as if to indicate to the President that he should continue to watch. The President turned his attention back to the scene.

Then there seemed to be a little movement. Among the trees and bushes there was a rock which had started to move sideways. It only moved about three feet and a light shone from behind this rock – a light that was rather dim at first but a light that became brighter and brighter.

"Ralph! What am I seeing here? Is this what I think it is Ralph? Ralph?"

Ralph was in a state of total shock and remained speechless. Suddenly there appeared what seemed to be two small comets with fiery tails swoop down from above and settle each side of the opening that was behind the rock. Then these two comet images took the shape of two bright but opaque figures, rather resembling blurry, translucent people. Ralph summoned a little nerve.

"Angels!"

Now the light emanating from behind the rock was very intense – almost too bright to look at, even on the footage. Then a figure appeared at the opening behind the rock, a figure of a man dressed in a blue and white cape which also shone so brightly. There was a halo of yellow light surrounding his head. The two attendants bowed to this man then attended his side, as he walked slowly forward, away from his tomb.

"My God! Is this what I think it is? Ralph?"

"It seems to be the resurrection of Jesus Christ, sir."

As the three figures moved forward away from the tomb and then out of view, the President tried to collect himself.

"Holy God – I don't believe it!"

"You don't believe in the resurrection of Jesus Christ, sir?"

"Yes Ralph I do but, I don't believe that I have just seen it - with my own eyes."

"I can't believe it either, sir. He is my Lord."

After a few minutes, a woman appeared at the tomb. She noticed that the rock had been moved, she skittishly peered inside then went into the tomb, re-appearing a minute or so later carrying a white cloth, but quickly running from the scene.

"Ralph, are you going to tell me that was Mary Magdalene?"

"Ah ... yes sir, I believe that would have been Mary Magdalene sir. She would have been told of Jesus' resurrection by an angel inside the tomb, sir."

"What was that she was carrying as she came out?"

"That would have been the Holy Shroud of Turin, Mr President."

"The Holy Shroud of Turin! You mentioned that before Ralph. Doesn't that still survive even today?"

"Yes sir, it is held in the Catholic Cathedral in the city of Turin, in Italy sir."

The footage came to an end, the President and his aides turned toward the Zircon leader and stood there totally stunned at what they had just witnessed, with tears still rolling down their faces, for about a half minute, then they bowed their approval. The President then stepped forward, took the Zircon leader by the right hand, kissed the back of his hand and emotionally said his thanks.

Zultan then motioned for the President and his aides to sit once again. He addressed the President about the nature of the world's religions and implored the President to convey his message to the people of the world. Zultan spoke for just twenty minutes, but he knew this President could take his message and elucidate upon it in many ways. They had come here at this time because of the inauguration of this particular United States President.

Zultan spoke of the world's religious movements and of his own people's spiritual evolution and how they had learned to be tolerant of each other and to understand the beliefs of all religious movements.

Zultan expressed that events occurring in the world today would be beneficial for a long time as the problem of terrorism was gradually brought under relative control and peace would be restored to most parts of the earth - until the time of the big calamity. The President queried Zultan on this but Zultan simply responded that this would be after the time of the President himself - and many more that succeed him – and closer to the end of the present century.

But it did not have to be this way!

Zultan divulged that our educationists would take up the challenge to explain major religious movements and how this would be conducive to the process of countering radical indoctrination. He explained how the United Nations would nurture a religious education movement that would attenuate dogmatism and lead to higher levels of understanding.

Zultan then disclosed that a major event that would facilitate religious unity included a future Catholic Pontiff who would discard the vow of celibacy for his priests and would allow his priests to marry and for married men to become priests. The same Pontiff would discard the concept of Papal infallibility and that this would lead the future King William of England, to accede the authority of his church to Rome. The young King William always remembered the words of his mother, Princess Diana – 'we all worship the same God and the establishment should get stuffed'. The unified Christian churches would release a comprehensive exposition denouncing dogmatism – within Christianity, Islam and all other major religious movements.

He also disclosed that an abundant amount of research had been conducted by them into near death experiences and after life experiences and that they had reason to fervently believe that death is merely a gateway to a greater life – a spiritual life in a state of existence that we would regard as being in Heaven. Zultan explained that people had been returned to life after extended periods of time in an apparent state of death and had testified that they had been able to traverse the entire universe in either distance or time. The Zircons had developed the technology that would allow people to recall such experiences, when they regained full cognizance.

Some people had told stories of how they witnessed the dinosaurs on earth and had also ventured into the future – that the space time of the universe was theirs to explore and to enjoy any way they desired. He stated that they believed this was a particular aspect of being in Heaven. Another sensation reported by such people was that of swimming in an ocean of love.

They believed that all good people will go to this place like Heaven, for ensconced within goodness is the golden rule – do unto others as you would have them do unto you. This is the foundation of their entire society.

But Zultan then described the circumstances of the great calamity and how everybody on Earth would need to work together and strive to avert this from happening. For the Zircons and others had been coming to Earth for a long time to avert many such calamities – such as the development of atomic weapons by the axis of evil many years before. They had shut down atomic weapons within the United States and the former Soviet Union because of an order given in the Soviet Union to initiate a nuclear war – that was based on a false alarm. Zultan did reveal, however, that despite all precautions there was always a possibility that terrorists could surreptitiously develop weapons of mass destruction and that social cooperation was the only way to prevent a nuclear holocaust.

Zultan gave the President details of how the human race would survive if we did not succeed in nurturing social cooperation here on Earth – on Mars!

The President was certainly intrigued about this but had to ask how the Zircons could know of the future events Zultan had referred to, that would occur here on earth.

Zultan then divulged to the President and to his two aides Ralph and Lynda, details that shocked them completely – the details of how they knew so much about our future.

Zultan explained that his people had colonized many planets in the far reaches of the Milky Way Galaxy and that they were also on a long journey to the Andromeda Galaxy and other galaxies too, within the Local Group and the Virgo Supercluster. Zultan then disclosed to the President and his two closest aides, where the Zircons had come from and why they had made their planet Zircon their base planet within the galaxy.

The President was totally shocked and initially in a state of disbelief by this final revelation, but this did explain so many things – about creation, the abundance of life in the universe, Jesus Christ and the role of the human race. The President knew he would need to be extremely prudent in explaining this revelation to the people of the world.

The Zircon high priests wished him well.

The Zircon leader and his two high priests then arose from their seats. Zultan handed the President the third gift – what seemed to be a rather tatty booklet of some type. They bowed to each other, the Zircons then turned to walk toward the doorway, as if to make their way back into their spacecraft, their mission being complete.

As they appeared from within the room and started to make their way back toward their spaceship, CXN's Rod Saunders picked up on the action from the CXN chopper.

"We have a new development taking place here now. It seems that our visitors are making their way back toward their spaceship, so perhaps they are preparing to leave us after this very short stay here on earth. You can see there that they are making their way up the landing gangway now. The President and his two closest aides are a short distance behind them. He also seems to have a small package placed under his arm, but wait, now he has stopped and is looking at the package which seems to be perhaps a small book of some kind. Now he is handing this item to his aide."

"Ralph, can you tell me what this is please?"

Ralph opened the book and quickly flicked through some pages. He was an erudite scholar and it did not take him long to glean the meaning of its contents.

"It is a book of technical specifications sir."

"Of what?"

"It seems to be about their propulsion systems sir."

"The President could not believe what he had just heard, for he knew that the course of humanity would be changed quite drastically forever now. For with this we human beings would be able to reach for the stars."

As the three Zircons reached the door of their ship, they turned and bowed to the President and his aides one last time, before the door closed. Only about thirty seconds later, the craft very slowly lifted off vertically from the roof of the building and then ascended with astonishing speed. Within just a few seconds, it was completely out of sight.

"Wow, would you look at that. They entered their spaceship, turned to say their goodbye and within a couple of seconds they are gone. Barbara!"

"That really is astonishing Rod, thank you so much for that footage of their leaving, but can you tell us where the President is now – does it look as though he is on his way back to the conference room?"

"Well, Barbara, no, right at the moment the President and his close aides are just standing there on the rooftop of the United Nations building looking upwards into the sky as if, perhaps, they can still see something. It … ah … looks as though the President and his two aides may in fact be weeping right now. This really is quite an extraordinary scene – the President has taken a handkerchief from his coat pocket and is wiping his eyes and now Lynda Lightfoot is doing the same. I have never seen anything like this before. You've got to wonder what on earth has taken place inside that room to bring this on. I certainly hope we can find out soon. Now the President has turned back toward the door and has placed his hands upon the shoulders of his two closest aides as if he is leading them back to the room but comforting them at the same time."

"Ralph! How do I explain this to the people?"

Chapter 13

Back in the studio CXN continued to consult the sociologist Professor David Jones.

"We have Professor David Jones back with us again and will continue our coverage of this extraordinary event here this morning on CXN as we await the next presentation for the President following his final meeting with our visitors who are here today from another planet within the Milky Way Galaxy. Professor Jones you wish to shed some more light on some of the, shall we say, confusing aspects of modern-day religion and on fundamentalism and cultism in particular so what can you tell us?"

"Barbara we have heard from quite a few people here this morning who might have upset a lot of people with talk of being saved from hell and so on but that is not surprising as religion can trap people into a doctrinal rut, you know, where they close off their minds to reason."

"Take the Pentecostal movement for example, given that the practice of tongues or glossolalia might actually be a total contrivance, one should ask why most of the Protestant Pentecostal Christians believe that all people who do not pray in tongues are to be damned for eternity – possibly even to a place called 'hell'. It is true that Catholic Pentecostals do not believe so, but the vast majority of Protestants Pentecostals Christians do."

"How would you know that?"

"We conducted research into this by asking the question 'do you believe that people who are not 'born again' will not be saved?' and found that more than eighty percent of Protestant Pentecostal Christians do believe that but only about five per cent of Catholic Pentecostals do."

"Why would there be such a huge difference between the Protestants and the Catholics?"

"It comes back to the authorities at the top and to the preachers who do the delivery of the doctrine – the Protestant ministers on one hand and the Catholic priests on the other.

The Assembly of God, for example, preaches this from the top as one of its fundamental truths whereas the Catholic Church shows far greater prudence in such things. To elaborate on that a little I would state that the Protestant evangelists are so comparatively dogmatic about the literal interpretation of the Gospel and particular verse from the Gospel, some of those we discussed earlier – such as 'no one goes to the Father except through me', which they take to mean that only Christians will go to heaven – and 'you must be born again' – which they assume is their experience – and they can be so totally flippant and dismissive of the eternal fate of anybody who does not fit that mold. This includes all non-Christians and all Christians who are not Pentecostal and profess to – or think they do but they don't – pray in tongues or, more correctly, practice glossolalia."

"The Catholic Church and its hierarchy within the Vatican are not so flippant – dare I express my own personal opinion and say – not so obtuse, or even not so stupid, as to believe that the almighty God who created the universe and everything within it would judge people he loves so infinitely, in a manner such as that."

"If you wish to see how some Protestant preachers portray the idea of a place they refer to as hell you need look no further than the paintings of 16th century Dutch artist Hieronymus Bosch. Many of them literally believe in hellfire and images of fourteen year old pregnant girls being cooked by demons, on a spit with a skewer running through their body from their genitals to their mouth, would gain concurrence from many of them, even most of them. The Catholic Church advocates that God is a loving God who may require some form of penance from people who live errant lives but there won't be any demonic figures cooking people on coals. Our modern view of scriptural reference to and to Jesus' reference to 'the fire that never goes out' is that hell might be a metaphorical reference to a protracted period of introspection for a reprehensible life – of knowing how one erred and the having to dwell within one's own mind separated from the love of God for a long time, but for how long, nobody knows."

"That is really interesting professor I have never heard of that artist, but your description sounds so way out I will first chance I get. Ah … can you tell me his name again please."

"Hieronymus Bosch. Don't worry Wikipedia has him covered, you'll find him quite easily and the paintings can be rather disturbing, but they do portray how most people would have thought of hell in previous centuries."

"And you have some more advice for us from the sociology of religion?"

"Yes you heard it said by the people from the Assembly of God that if a person recites the prayer that Mr. Pokelyn recited earlier today and give their life to Jesus, they will be saved. Now this reference to being 'saved' is a peculiarity of Protestantism and Pentecostalism in particular and within the parlance of the sociology of religion, as a discipline, we equate this aspect to it as being a part of the 'magic' in religion. The Pentecostals believe that in that very instant a person goes from being virtually damned for all eternity in hell, to being saved by Jesus and deserving of a place in heaven. So it equates to the waving of a magic wand over the person and changing them into something that they were not, even though there is not necessarily any profound transformation in the person's character at that point and the extent to which they are going to live up to that commitment is yet to be seen."

"So hypothetically you could have a murderous bank robber recite the prayer in good faith and immediately they are saved – for which, of course, there is a scriptural basis – Jesus made it clear to the criminal who was crucified with him that he would be in paradise that day. He also told the parable of the vineyard workers who came in at the last moment receiving the same reward as those who had been there all day. But where they go wrong with this is that they tend to treat this profound commitment quite flippantly as if simply getting someone to utter the words does the magic trick, without any great personal decision taking place. So you will hear them say things like or 'when I was saved' or 'on the day that I was saved'. Secondly, this level of commitment is what Jesus sought from the rich young man to become perfect – not to be saved. He was already on his way to heaven."

"Many of the people who are enticed into reciting this prayer, supposedly to go from being destined for hell into heaven, are also very good people who are already bound for eternal life in heaven. It's just that the Pentecostals don't believe those people are on their way to heaven and are in need of being saved. Finally, most mainstream Christian churches avoid using this term 'saved' because it implies that other really good people are not saved. The use of the term also reinforces the hegemony among the Pentecostals that they are the only true Christians, which of course is far from being true."

"So Professor you think that Pentecostal Christians should refrain from using that terminology?"

"Yes because it is misleading them, but that probably serves the purpose of their preachers very well and it conveys and upholds that aspect of magic within the religion."

"Yes it does seem rather extreme doesn't it?"

"Barbara, within the parlance of the social sciences we employ a concept that we refer to as 'the continuum'. If you take any social aspect that includes beliefs or attitudes or doctrine, you can plot or depict the location of a person's or an organization's position along the continuum between two opposite extremes. Now in the case of religious doctrine the two extremes might be regarded as exclusivist and inclusivist, or conservative and liberal. Dogmatism and religious exclusivity lie at the conservative end of the continuum whereas non-dogmatic or inclusive views of religious beliefs lie at the liberal end of the continuum."

"So typically when it comes to interpretation of scripture, such as the Gospel, dogmatic Pentecostal preachers will use scriptural verse to justify a position of exclusivity – they will proclaim, for example, that only born again Christians who have accepted Jesus Christ as their personal Lord and savior and have been baptized with the Holy Spirit of God and can evidence that with the gift of tongues will be 'saved' – as they put it – to heaven. The Jehovah's Witnesses adopt a similar disposition – they believe that only Jehovah's Witnesses will be saved to either heaven or paradise. They have a verse from St Paul's letter that refers to the early Christians as being witnesses so they believe that by naming themselves Jehovah's Witnesses they somehow become the ones that St Paul refers to – despite the totally dubious and spurious doctrine they preach."

"Are you sure you can be so definitive about referring to their doctrine as spurious?"

"Oh absolutely, they are definitely out there on a limb of their own, make no mistake about that - virtually every other Christian organization or church would subscribe to that statement."

"What ... including the Mormon church?"

"Well, yes, but they are out on a limb in a similar way, perhaps just not quite so far, with their dogmatism. They can be somewhat coy regarding their doctrine on the eternal fate of other Christians, but they are just as dogmatic regarding the fate of non-Christians. They do have some fundamental differences with the Jehovah's Witnesses regarding the deity or otherwise of Jesus, the state of the afterlife in heaven, the origins of the human soul and others areas too."

"And at the liberal end of this ... ah ... continuum?"

"Yes, the inclusive doctrines, probably exemplified and epitomized by the Baha'i faith that preaches unity among all religions and humanities – a type of common unity in the quest to be re-united with God. As such Buddhism too would be at this end of the continuum and of the mainstream Christian churches, probably the Catholic Church is the closest to this liberalism, by virtue of its doctrines such as the 'Anonymous Christian' and its stated acceptance and acknowledgement of Islam since the proclamation of Nostra Aetate by Vatican II, as being a part of God's church on earth."

"So are you suggesting that there is cultism in the mix here at the exclusivist end of the spectrum?"

"That is well put Tom, for it is not as appropriate to refer to religious movements as cults per se than to state that they have cultist traits because traits occur in varying degrees. Cultist movements often have similar themes and characteristics – an assertive, dominant, charismatic founder who is intensely venerated by followers, the production of special revelation or books unique to them – such as the Book of Mormon - authoritarian leadership, a belief in being the only "true" church, a sense of persecution by other religious groups, secret, distinctive language and vocabulary, exclusiveness, esoteric beliefs such as milk before meat and shunning government and family. You'll find these qualities in various combinations and degrees in Scientology, the Amish, the Jehovah's Witnesses, the Mormon church and others and historically even more-so among the Hare Krishna's, the Branch Davidians, the Heaven's Gate people and the Jonestown sect in Guyana in 1978. Obviously, some of the latter groups can be regarded purely as cults whereas others need to be regarded as religious movements with some cultist traits."

"And Islam?"

"No! You cannot label Islam as a cult - it is a religion and has been acknowledged as such by the Catholic Church several decades ago to distinguish Islam from Buddhism and Hinduism. But it does have some cultist aspects to it – such as preventing all Islamic people from converting to any other form of religious belief such as Christianity or Hinduism and there is, of course, a lot of geographical overlap between Islam and Hinduism and Buddhism in nations like Pakistan and India. So that type of persecution of any form of apostasy is cultist. It is also cultist to ban people from believing in the Trinity as most Christians do. Religious belief systems should not ban people from believing such things, because ultimately nobody knows the truth."

"Wow, Professor Jones thank you for that contribution, I am sure that your rendition there clarifies a lot of the confusion that many people would be feeling about some of the religious or cultist movements that we know of."

"Now we welcome back our special social commentator New York's top morning radio host Mr. Zach Ferodo via video link from New York. Zach you have some more interesting commentary to add to our discussion here today."

"Yes thank you once again Barbara, there are three things I wish to say now that I have been able to do a little research since completing my on-air stint. Firstly, I had a brief look at the websites of the Scientologists and that Bible Discernment Ministry, who I had never heard of previously and I have got to say, I find the information and the doctrine there to be so really weird, that my advice to people is to stay away from those places. It's no wonder that so many people seem to be brainwashed by religious beliefs."

"In my work at 2NY I have always tried to be very tactful, diplomatic, rather circumspect and even prudent in the way that I present things but I have got to say that in some things now I just have to call a spade a spade, you know, for everybody's sake. Because some of your guests themselves have been rather prudent on what they have said and that is quite understandable, especially on a day such as this you don't want to go out there and just blow people's religious beliefs out of the water. But I have just got to follow up on some things that have been said. It is an unfortunate aspect of religion here in the United States that some people do read their Bible and whether it is out of ego or vanity or pride or one-upmanship or malice or spite or grandstanding, far too many people contrive a doctrine that is so totally spurious as to be farcical."

"I suppose the best or the worst of these we have seen today would be from that Bible Discernment representative and his rendition here today clearly exemplifies what I mean. Did anybody here make any sense of that stuff, at all? No! I had never heard of the Bible Discernment Ministry before this morning but since I was on air earlier I took the trouble of looking at its website and, I have got to say it, those people are both weird and wacky. That is the weirdest stuff I have ever read in my entire life, though I suppose a few other cults might give them a run for their money. But I see what the sociologist and the bishop mean when they very diplomatically refer to misinterpretation of the scripture and using the scripture to support a doctrine when any nexus between the doctrine and the scripture being cited is so totally dubious. The conclusion of the Bible Discernment group is that all non-Christians and most Christians too are damned for eternity, because they do not subscribe to his teaching – that is Mr. Rick himself. Which really has to be some of the most dogmatic - supposedly Christian - doctrine I have ever heard."

"I think the priests have been rather generous in their treatment of some of our Pentecostal friends too. I took a quick look at some of the basic tenets of the Assembly of God and the scriptural reference to support their line that only born again Christians will be 'saved' (motions with his fingertips) is just as dubious. And I see where the psychologist is coming from now because some of the doctrine that AOG is peddling there is so blatantly vindictive - toward Muslim people in particular but generally toward anybody who is not a so-called born-again Christian. Which pleases me greatly to have heard here today, for the very first time, a clarification of the Gospel and that term 'born again' that has been bandied around for many decades now, in many Pentecostal Christians claiming to be 'saved' and that everybody else is damned. I am so pleased to know that their belief is based on such a spurious interpretation of what Jesus meant when he said that. And while I am on the Assembly of God, let me call a spade a spade, some of those evangelists are just money shylocks – they were people of God until the money took them over and now the only God they serve is money."

"Secondly, as a Christian person myself I was brought up by my parents within the Baptist Church believing in creationism and their belief was that God created everything in seven solar days – or was it six days then he rested on the seventh – whichever it was, about seven thousand years ago, but as I became further educated, just as your Professor Jones said, I started to accept that evolution had taken place over millions of years. So I suppose I reverted to accepting that because at college there were just so many highly educated and qualified people who took it for granted that evolution had taken place over a very long time. I mean, the idea of young-earth creationism was a total no brainer for anybody studying the sciences of biology or geology."

"But then as I became aware of the debate raging within the school system many years ago when the creationists resorted to touting the concept of intelligent design, I ... ah ... began to re-consider and thought, well maybe there is a type of composite solution or a compromise here. I mean, if you follow the argument put forward by Dr. Valmai Green earlier, as espoused also by Sir David Attenborough, that every living species today is the final survivor of a long series of less successful species, where are all the fossil remains of those half-baked species?"

"If you take everybody's favorite the T-Rex for example, paleontologists have discovered dozens of fossilized remains of the fully developed T-Rex, but where are all the remains of the dinosaurs that lived that evolved into the T-Rex? According to the theory there should be many more unsuccessful species of T-Rex than the final product. So I wonder whether the road that species have taken in that succession has been guided by an almighty deity to take the short road to grandma's house rather than the long road. Of course, I still do subscribe to the theory of evolution but perhaps God played more of a role in that than the scientists are prepared to acknowledge."

"That's an interesting angle you place on that Zach and I suspect a lot of people on both sides of the fence would agree. And there was something else?"

"Yes Tom, this might come as quite a surprise to most people but when I was at college in my early twenties I did meet a young lady there, a fellow student of journalism who became my first girlfriend and she was a Pentecostal Christian, from within my church, the local Baptist Church. She had quite a profound influence on me and I couldn't understand her exuberance for her relationship with God so she took me along to a meeting and people prayed over me and in that situation I made a decision that, yes, I would devote my life to God. So they got me to recite the prayer of accepting Jesus as personal Lord and savior and then they all congratulated me and gave me hugs and kisses and then we started to sing songs and everybody was doing the 'happy clapper' thing so I joined in and I must admit I did feel quite some release ... ah ... none of the usual inhibitions that I might have previously felt."

"But the most amazing thing occurred the next day, when I went outside into the open air to take the ride to college. The train went by the river and the forest and it was a beautiful clear day with a stunning blue sky and it occurred to me that I really was seeing everything for the very first time. The colors of God's creation were so overwhelmingly beautiful I couldn't believe what I was seeing and I remember thinking to myself 'why haven't I seen this before?' I remember thinking to myself 'how can this possibly exist?' and 'why can't everybody else see this the way that I do now' and I had a talk to one of the pastors about this and he said that was the common experience of people who are baptized in the Spirit – that they see the wonders of God's creation for the first time. He read to me the verse from Saint Paul's letter to the Romans, I think it is chapter eight verse twenty eight, that we are able to perceive God's eternal power and divine glory in the things that he has made. I must admit, however, that in later years I have not really been able to experience that same awe in God's creation that I did so many years ago."

"So I do understand why people who are so-called 'born again' believe that they are so close to God and that other people are not, but having said that, I do accept the explanation of Professor Jones and Cardinal Gilroy that those born again Christians have responded to God in the way that Jesus challenged the rich young man."

"Thank you for sharing that with us today Zach, I am sure that a lot of people will pay heed to what you have said based on your own personal experience there. Now Zach while we still have you here, please tell us what you think about this, supposing these aliens have made contact with the government of the USA and if this has been occurring for some time, even decades, is there any conceivable valid reason for the level of suppression of disclosure that has taken place?"

"Oh absolutely - there could be many reasons for that pertaining not only to the implications for religious beliefs but to national security and international security, it could be that weapons systems have been compromised, we might have been advantaged in some way over perceived adversaries such as the former Soviet Union, we don't know if China is working toward an ulterior objective for military domination via contamination of computer systems, E.T. might have blessed the USA with intelligence that would provide it with a distinct advantage over any adversary, so the reasons are quite profound."

"Why us and not the others?"

"Well they would certainly be aware of what happened in the two world wars and who was who doing what and of the atrocities that were perpetrated by the axis of evil and of the underlying distrust of communism in suppressing and oppressing people. Consider Stalin and his genocide of twenty million of his own people or the modern day North Korea where millions of people die every year from starvation while the economy props up a lavish military to oppress the people. Suffice to say that E.T. would know the good guys from the baddies! On the other hand E.T. might have disclosed powerful weapons systems to many nations for the purpose of maintaining an equilibrium where no powerful nation could gain ascendancy or a more likely scenario would be that E.T.

might have demonstrated the folly of our weapons and conflict because they could shut everything down. As we have heard on Dr. Steven Greer's Disclosure Project, this might have happened already, so the people would perceive that our governments are not in control of our own weapons systems."

"I mean, we have heard from a succession of Presidents who all say the same thing and some of those – Jimmy Carter in particular but also Ronald Reagan and Bill Clinton – were so intent on providing the public with disclosure. In fact the question was put to Mr. Obama recently by Jimmy Kimmel and even he was somewhat coy and flippant in his response in that he virtually laughed it off saying that 'I can't reveal anything' and 'the aliens won't let it happen' and 'we would reveal all their secrets' and 'they exercise strict control over us' and when Jimmy Kimmel quoted Bill Clinton saying that there is nothing there, Mr. Obama stated 'well that's what we're instructed to say'. But reading between the lines this was exactly his semantical way of confirming that, yes, the United States government is in ongoing discourse with aliens and is under instruction to keep a lid on this."

"One former CIA agent divulged everything that he encountered when he was sent to Area 51 by former President Dwight D. Eisenhower, after Eisenhower was informed by the head honcho at Area 51 that the US government had no jurisdiction over Area 51. The President threatened to virtually invade Area 51 with the First National Army, so the CIA agents were given the royal tour of all of the spacecraft that had been secured and one living extra-terrestrial being who survived the Roswell crash. Now when you couple this with the evident advanced technology that can shut down missile facilities, obviously the US government is going to play ball with the aliens."

"So President Obama's jovial responses were his way of letting people know the truth, without being seen to be too blatant or even derelict about it. The US government probably does have strict instructions from alien civilizations. It becomes a question of how the world's societies and the social cohesion attributable to religious beliefs would stand up to the revelation of extra-terrestrial life in the universe."

"So thank you Barbara for inviting me to come back here today."

"Zach thank you for dropping by again to give us an update on your thoughts and, well, thank goodness that you were able to do a little research there for us today because I believe that does shed quite some light on the subject."

Chapter 14

"Now we understand that the President will be with us shortly to ... ah ... once again address the nation, perhaps for the final time about this morning's extraordinary events and, hopefully, he will bring us more good news. Tom what are you thinking right now?"

"Well the President will, of course, be addressing people all over the world, there would not be a single nation out there with the television technology that would not be tuned into this, so no doubt people of all religious persuasions are going to be very anxious about this. We have heard from a number of religious leaders here this morning and some are telling us this is the return of the Lord and the end of times and others are being more open minded, so I certainly hope they are on the money, because I don't want today to be the last day of human existence."

"Okay the President has returned to the media room and is preparing his final address here now."

The television coverage returns to the media room where the President had taken up his position at the podium. The ambience was one of somber anticipation as everybody was totally transfixed as the President began to speak.

"My fellow Americans, people of the world. Today I bring you even more good news. As you know our friends who visited us here today have left already, after being with us for just a few short hours, but I can tell you that what they have disclosed here today will give all of us profound hope for a better future for humanity."

"They asked us to ponder the way that we have evolved as a species from an ancestor that was common to all primates some several millions of years ago. We ... ah ... evolved through a progression of initially ape-like creatures such as

Pithecanthropus and Australopithecus to modern day homo-sapiens and these changes took several millions of years."

"Now for those of you who have long held the belief that God created the world in seven solar days as accounted for in the book of Genesis, let me assure you that God did create the world, but a long, long time ago. The account of creation as portrayed in the book of Genesis must now be seen by all, for its metaphorical presentation of the creation of ... ah ... not only our world but indeed, of the entire universe."

"God has given us various gifts with which we can get to understand him better. Our scientists are gifted people who have taken strident steps in explaining our world, our galaxy, our universe. Thanks to our development of the Hubble telescope and others too, we have a far better understanding now of just how massive the universe really is and also of how old the universe is. I believe the commonly accepted age is more than thirteen and a half billion years. This is when God created the universe and our world - our planet Earth - has been developed by a myriad of forces that have made up our solar system in more recent times – probably in the last five billion years."

"So to those of you who have held to the belief that God created the world about seven thousand years ago, I say do not despair, for I do have some very good news."

"Our friends who came here today look the way they do because, as we said earlier, they come from a planet far smaller than Earth but so much brighter too. Hence, they are considerably smaller than us and have developed eyes to protect themselves from the glare of their sun. They have inhabited their planet for about twenty-two thousand years and have had to adapt to its environment."

"But what they have divulged here to us today gives me tremendous hope that we human beings do in fact survive and prosper. Now, do not be too alarmed at what I am about to tell you and please ... just give me a chance to explain further, okay."

"Our visitors from the planet Zircon have revealed to us today that they are, in fact ... us from our future."

"Huh?"

This comment caused immediate confusion and consternation all over the world – people were making various groans of incredulity and consulting each other for the views of another.

"This can't be true!"

"How can we evolve to look like that?"

"They are so ugly!"

"Shit no!"

"Now I know what a lot of you are thinking so I need to clarify this. They are a small part of us from one colony in our future! But let me be quick to assure you and to placate you, that in that future time, most of us do not actually look like them, no, we look just the way we are here today, for our genetics have been preserved on many planets in the Milky Way Galaxy. In fact, in our future it could be said that we look even more beautiful that we do today, for the human race has been evolving to look increasingly beautiful. We all know that beauty is a subjective assessment and that beauty is truly in the eyes of the beholder. But I don't think too many people would disagree that your typical Neanderthal woman was not quite as beautiful as Claudia Schiffer!"

Once again everybody laughed!

After a moment of contemplation, the President scratched his head and qualified this comment.

"Or my wife!"

Everybody laughed again.

"These particular future humans who have come here today are leaders in the future human race and they have selected their planet Zircon as their base because it is well endowed with the element 115 which does allow them to harness the power of ... ah ... ubiquitous gravitational waves. This power allows them to travel at a speed approaching the speed of light squared. I say ubiquitous because they have divulged that this gravitational force is everywhere at all times and is moving in every conceivable direction simultaneously, hence the force of gravity is the very fabric of space-time. As such it is able to maintain solar systems in place, even though planets like Pluto are such a long way from their parent star. Gravitational waves are a type of omnipresent force."

"This particular colony from Zircon are involved in extracting and processing this very rare element for human colonies in the entire galaxy. They have, of course, been coming here for many decades in recent times, in their experimental phases where they have had to send droids and other craft - that we have come to know as unidentified flying objects - because of the distortions that take place with travel through space time."

"Did you hear that – that these aliens who have been coming here for decades are us from our future?"

The President continued.

"These particular human beings have come here today from their planet Zircon, where they have had to evolve to their present-day appearance, out of necessity. As I said earlier their planet is smaller than our planet Earth and very much brighter. But they are just one of many divergent colonies of human beings that colonize the Milky Way Galaxy. They have managed to come here from a point of time in our future, some twenty thousand years from now. They have divulged that we human beings, in their time, just twenty-two thousand years from now, are established on more than seventy planets within our Milky Way galaxy."

"The Zircon people are our future leaders and governors. They have aspects of technology that they do not disclose to all human colonies for reasons pertaining to security but are closely guarded by the Intergalactic Council. Some of the ... ah ... politics of George Lucas' Star Wars would ring true with most of you on that score. The technologies they safeguard could be equated to how we, ourselves, are today with weapons of mass destruction – that we keep that technology in safe hands. Their planet Zircon is extremely well guarded and virtually impregnable. It is also a haven for the most intelligent human beings, so the pursuit of scientific knowledge is based at Zircon. We could equate that to our own Silicon Valley here in the USA."

"Fortunately, with the technology they are able to discover new habitable planets on an ongoing basis and are able to establish new colonies of human civilizations on a regular basis. Hence there will come a point of time, in our own history, when there will no longer be any need for human beings to be fighting each other over land or resources. We will all have as much as we need, even as much as we want."

"They have estimated that it will take thousands of years for them to completely explore all of the galaxies within our Virgo supercluster. For those of you who do not know very much about this, our galaxy the Milky Way and the Andromeda Galaxy are the two largest galaxies in a system comprised of about forty galaxies, known as the Virgo supercluster. The smaller galaxies within this intergalactic neighborhood of ours probably contain just one hundred million stars. This might sound like a lot of stars, but our Milky Way galaxy has more than three hundred billion stars and possibly as many as four hundred billion stars. The Andromeda galaxy has perhaps three times as many. Then it will take them many months of space travel to reach the next nearest group of galaxies. We could liken this process to the opening up of the interior of the USA or of our west, back in the eighteenth century. It will be a long slow process but one that they are excited about."

"Our friends are hopeful that in the not-too-distant future they will make another breakthrough in space and time travel that might allow them to traverse the universe much more quickly. Their best mathematical minds are working on several strategies already that involve worm holes, dark energy and even black holes. Their latest theories postulate the concept of dark gravity that just might allow intergalactic travel at virtually unlimited speeds. We here on earth still have no idea what gravity is - except that it causes apples to fall from trees!"

"Now you must all be wondering if and when our friends, our futuristic human being of one kind, are going to bless us with some technology that will assist our cause in traversing space. They have said that they will assist us at some time in the future but that we need to do some sorting out here for ourselves first. Of paramount importance, we must begin to understand each other's beliefs. We must do everything we can to overcome the bigotry that is so rife within our world. Christians need to understand the beliefs of Islamic people and Muslim people need to understand that Christians believe that Jesus is the Son of God who rose from the dead to save all of us."

"On this I need to now divulge to you, something that is so amazing as to be almost totally unbelievable – something that was disclosed to us here this morning. Our visitors come from their planet, Zircon, a little more than two thousand and twenty light years away. Hence the light that left our planet Earth some two thousand and nineteen years ago is still on its way travelling through space toward their planet. With their technology, of course, they have been able to move closer to Earth to, in fact, view events that occurred here on earth two thousand and twenty five years ago. They have been able to take up a position in space and observe events that took place here at that time."

"Now, the purity of light travelling through space is such that it does not deteriorate – rather it maintains its intensity and strength and its purity. It does not become attenuated or diluted in any way. Of course, with their far advanced technology they have been able to record events that took place here on earth thousands of years ago. By now most of you would be familiar with the beautiful images of deep space that we have been able to compile using our Hubble and Spitzer telescopes and we are hoping to enhance such images with the James Webb telescope this year. We were all blown away when we saw the first images of deep space using the Hubble, what we named the Hubble Deep Space View. Well, suffice to say, as you might expect, that the technology of the Zircon people, being some twenty-two thousand years from our future, is even far more advanced than what we could imagine. That is the way of scientific progress."

"So with their technology our friends from Zircon have been able to record events that took place here on earth on the twenty fifth of April in the year zero."

"That was the day that our Lord Jesus Christ was crucified."

Everybody in the entire world was shocked! The succinct utterances were numerous and varied.

"Huh!"

"Did you hear that?"

"That's gotta be bullshit!"

"I don't believe it!"

"My God – I knew it! Praise the Lord!"

"And today our friends from Zircon have been able to replay the images of that event, the crucifixion of Jesus Christ, for us - for I have seen this with my own eyes."

"Huh!"

"I'll believe that when I see it with *my* own eyes!"

This was the news that completely shocked the world – it shocked everybody in the world, all in a single moment. The impact on everybody was profound, people were totally exasperated, for regardless of whether they were Christian or Muslim or Hindu or Buddhist or Taoist or agnostic or atheist or just plain ignorant, the implications of this were so totally astounding. Everybody knew of Jesus Christ and everybody knew that he had claimed to be the Son of God and everybody knew that according to the Christian gospel he had risen from the dead on the third day of his passion, so that we might all be able to return to God. The moment was not lost on anybody, anywhere. It was as if in a single instant, the truth about all religious ideas was about to be revealed.

And it was!

"People of the world! I am here to inform you that on this day, I, the President of the United States of America and my two closest aides Ralph and Lynda, were blessed with being able to view the events of that day, the passion of Jesus Christ, the scourging at the pillar, the crucifixion of Jesus and his mother and his disciples standing at the foot of the cross as he died."

"But even more significantly, we were then shown the most extraordinary event in human history, for we witnessed the glorious resurrection of our Lord Jesus Christ from the tomb, less than two days later."

Everybody in the entire world was stunned, completely shocked, for this was a life-changing moment for every person. The world would never be the same again.

"We have been blessed by our friends with a device that has this record intact – and we intend to release this for everybody to see, with your own eyes. This is a genuine historical record of events that took place at that time – the most important moments in the history of humanity. We will, in due course allow everybody to witness these events for themselves, as we will make these images freely available to everyone."

"The Zircon people have done this to assist us to avoid a cataclysmic tragedy that we were heading towards – a world where war became an ongoing daily event, a war that was based on a confusion of political and religious ideas and beliefs."

"Many of you would be familiar with the words 'no fate but what we make' which was, of course, popularized in a well-known film, Terminator 2. Well there is a lot of truth in that and our friends have come here today from our future to try to steer us in a different direction. For they, themselves, were among the last survivors of humanity who lived in an outpost on the planet Mars, from where they were able to implement the technology that took them to a succession of other planets before they settled at the planet Zircon. They have taken the opportunity to come here again, they have come backwards in time, with a technology that has been given to them, to give us all a second chance."

"They have disclosed the timing of the calamity that we face in the not-too-distant future, so we must all begin to cooperate with each other in understanding our varied beliefs, in the way we treat this planet, our only home, in further dismantling of our weapons systems and in overcoming the abject poverty that too many of our people are forced to endure."

"Now some of what I am about to divulge to you, I may be referring to in the past tense – as if it has already happened, even though it is still in our future. This is because our visitors here today do come from our future and the events of which I am going to speak are in their past. I hope that makes sense to you all. I must warn you that many of you will find this rather shocking and I reiterate that without their intervention here today, this pathway of destruction is where we just might be heading."

228

"In the years some time ahead of us we will make quite a mess of this planet, Earth – our home. Global warming will lead to the demise of coral reefs, of frogs and other amphibians, of bees and then, of course, species of vegetation that relied on bees and other insects for pollination. That vegetation will include certain of our food crops – vegetables, fruit and grain crops. We will face a dire shortage of food and this will lead to anarchy in many parts of the world. The problem of terrorism will once again become quite pronounced and in several middle east and African nations there will be virtually no law and order at all. Hordes of marauding terrorists will wreak havoc in large parts of the globe, pillaging and plundering and inflicting massive terrorist attacks on thousands of innocent people in western countries. Nobody will be safe. Eventually, they will secure nuclear weapons and destroy many of the world's largest cities. The contamination will cause further degradation of the world's food producing areas and food will be in short supply."

We went so far with our destruction of this planet Earth – our only home – with our exploitation of fossil fuels that had such adverse effects on our environment – which was something that this planet had never experienced before, because no species of animal had ever previously been able to perpetrate such effects - that our planet went into shutdown mode. Mother Nature decided it was time to protect her environment and for the first time in more than eleven thousand years, she initiated the next ice age."

In the winter of the year 2099, the snowfalls that normally covered Canada then the northern states of the United States of America as well as northern parts of the Asian land mass including Siberia and Russia and Norwegian nations too, progressed to an extent of coverage that we had never witnessed before. The snowfalls of that year started later than usual by several weeks, as if Mother Nature was delaying the onset of the winter to stockpile her deluge, but when it started, it would not stop. Within two weeks many cities and metropolitan areas had been completely covered in snow that was so deep that emergency services could not operate - period. In fact even emergency personnel were progressively trapped so deeply within areas in their endeavors to rescue thousands of citizens that they too were unable to extricate themselves and inevitably perished, in ever-increasing numbers. By the time we realized what was happening in Alaska and Canada, extensive areas of the USA, Asia and Europe were already going under. The southernmost parts of South America, too, were inundated with snow and ice."

"Niagara Falls froze over in less than one day and in just four days this city of New York, Chicago, Seattle and San Francisco became buried under snow so deep that these entire cities and all of their utilities of power and water and then their populations were lost. This situation progressed southwards much faster than we could have anticipated and within days the mid-west of the USA and southern Europe including Great Britain and cities such as Peking, Beijing and Tokyo, were all inundated with snow."

"By this time New York City and all areas north of that latitude were under hundreds of feet of snow, which was compacting into ice. Tens of millions of people perished within one week. Even places such as Los Angeles could not prevent the inevitable, as masses of people were trying to evacuate and causing total mayhem in their endeavors to stockpile food, fuel and other necessities of life and to head south toward Mexico."

"Within a week of the situation becoming totally irretrievable, our Capital city Washington D.C. too, was engulfed under snow and ice, by which time New York City was buried beneath more than three hundred feet of ice. Needless to say that any people trapped in that situation perished. The United States administration had no choice but to abandon the United States to take refuge in the one place where we could be certain that we would not be consumed by snow and a place that was receptive to our governance. That place, of course, was Australia, the land of friendly people - who put beetroot on their hamburgers!"

Some people laughed!

"We then evacuated as many people as we could to Australia and established an administration center in the city of Darwin. From there we had to do everything we could to ensure the safety of the world's remaining non-hostile governments, to prevent errant-minded forces taking control over nations that would survive the ice age. As terrorist organizations tried to commandeer the governments of many nations in the middle-east, in northern Africa and other parts of Africa and South America, we held a military and administrative stronghold in Darwin, from where we had reasonable access to other parts of the surviving world."

"So our friends from Zircon have warned us that we do not have to suffer this fate, but in order to avert the onset of this Ice Age we need to do more to implement the Treaty signed by nations in Paris in December 2015 to sever our reliance on fossil fuels and to fully implement a reliance on renewable energy. Mother Nature will not wait for us on this. We need the political will to dictate terms to the vested interests of the carbon producing fuel suppliers – our oil companies and our coal mining companies – that we need to avert this impending cataclysm that will inflict our future generations."

"As this situation is developing, we become even more intent upon establishing a human outpost on Mars. NASA had already located the position of flowing water in various areas of Mars over many years and was able to successfully drill for water to make the establishment of a colony viable and feasible. In between the years 2050 and 2060 we do construct a second space station that utilizes ion propulsion and is able to make the journey to Mars – albeit over a period of more than twelve months - and settle in orbit above the red planet, much like our space station above the earth. We achieve this with a new version of the space shuttle that is the size of a 747 jet airliner and, as such, will be able to convey substantial amounts of materials into space. This space station will initially be equipped with hundreds of robotic workers each programmed to undertake a specific task and are able to manufacture carbon fiber panels utilizing the planets own minerals."

"This space station will be about the size of two present-day submarines adjoined by a central module such that the entire construction is capable of rotating for the purpose of providing gravity, as this was deemed to be an imperative for such a journey if people were to follow. Over a period of twenty years the robots are able to construct fully self-contained shelter and greenhouses that are suitable for producing vegetable and fruit crops within those greenhouses. The robots also establish the infrastructure for the extraction of water from the red planet."

"During these initial phases there are no humans on Mars – the plan being to establish as much infrastructure as possible before we send any people there. We are able to send forth quite a great range of materials and equipment to the space station orbiting Mars as the space station is capable of returning to its Earth orbit. The space station is also equipped with the machinery to allow items to be transported to the surface – such as helium balloons, parachutes and rocket thrusters. Some of the equipment taken to Mars is for the purpose of extracting minerals on Mars, which was undertaken using highly specialized robots that managed to stockpile large quantities of metals and carbon fiber that would be needed to build new spacecraft."

"Then we eventually send fifty couples to Mars to become our first ever inter-planetary humans out-posted away from planet Earth. All of these couples are volunteers and are very well educated and highly skilled. They take with them some chickens, some rabbits, some goats and some fish to allow them to cultivate animals for protein and milk and dairy foods and to implement a balance with the vegetable and fruit crops. They also took some very intelligent but placid breeds of dogs, such as golden retrievers, German shepherds, silky terriers, border collies and the Australian kelpie, purely for the purpose of providing the people with affection. The dogs were of critical importance in providing stress relief for the people on Mars. They took no cats and no rats. Oh, but they also took some budgerigars to ensure that somebody was always on hand to talk to the dogs – which they did incessantly. Needless to say, that for this occupied journey the gravity rotation function of the space station was activated as this was deemed to be an imperative for such a long journey – especially for the budgies."

Everybody laughed! The importance of some subtle humor to placate a tentative world was not lost on this President.

"This part of the experiment proved to be highly successful and it will allow the first settlers to survive and to perpetuate even more infrastructure for the extraction of crucial minerals and for food production. Upon arrival at Mars, one woman gave birth to a child – a son - the very first human being to be born on another planet."

The President continued with a wry smile.

"She named her son Adam."

Some people laughed!

"Adam was, appropriately, born on the first day of January in the year 2100 and this has been recorded as such – though they believe they will need a new calendar on Mars. It takes a lot longer for Mars to revolve around the Sun that Earth does,

233

so their year is much longer. Another pioneer found herself pregnant with a soon to be born daughter and decided that her daughter would be named Eve."

Everybody laughed!

"In case you are wondering – yes Adam and Eve do eventually get married - to each other. However, I do digress."

"Subsequent journeys to the red planet with the space station allowed us to take many other species of animals to Mars, such as horses, cattle, sheep and poultry, as well as many more people. Sounds a little like a future Noah's Ark!"

"During this entire period of time our scientists make considerable progress towards calculating how to travel faster than the speed of light, as we are fairly sure that we might have to leave Earth or Mars at some point of time in the future and head for planets in other parts of the Milky Way Galaxy. As the situation here on earth becomes more and more critical, we ramp up our efforts to crack the code for space-time travel and it will be a physics and mathematics student from the Tai Poutini Polytechnic in Greymouth, New Zealand who postulates a theoretical equation that provides us with the big breakthrough. Her one-inch long equation is somewhat similar to that utilized by these Zircon visitors that enables them to travel a speed almost as fast as the speed of light squared. She seemingly did this with a computer program that calculated the number of possible symbols that such an equation could possibly be comprised of and then implemented every possible combination and permutation with these symbols until the program arrived at the desired answer. In other words, she virtually solved this equation by working it backwards."

"Paradoxically, it was just as we developed this major breakthrough that things deteriorate to the point of no return here on earth, with the inception of the demise of numerous species of trees."

"Obviously without trees, we cannot live – we do not live. We then frantically dispense hundreds more couples to the Mars outpost over a period of two years in case we could not retrieve the situation here on earth."

"And so the Mars outpost becomes our number one hope for the future of humanity. We did place extremely stringent controls in place on Mars to ensure that ... ah ... we did not make the same mistakes with the Martian environment that we made here on Earth. No cats – no rats!"

"With our extraction of the hydrogen molecule from the water on Mars, coupled with an abundance of carbon on the red planet, one by-product of our activities on Mars will be the production of copious amounts of carbon dioxide. Being a relatively heavy gas the carbon dioxide tended to stay closer to the Martian surface while it disperses, than it would on Earth. This will give us great hope of one day terraforming the red planet, using select plants to produce oxygen. With that in mind, a select group of families will make the brave and bold decision to leave that planet and for head for the stars, knowing it could take more than two years before they located a suitable habitat."

"But this they do – a planet just eight light years from Earth, a planet they named Utopia. This planet is smaller than Earth with uninhabitable polar regions, but a relatively narrow section of this planet near its equator was habitable. Utopia was also blessed with the range of minerals we have here on earth. Once this colony was formed, other people followed. It is on this planet of Utopia that the human race survived and prospered for a sufficiently long period of time, to allow further expeditions to other parts of the Milky Way Galaxy and lead our friends here today from the planet Zircon, to make that planet their home for many thousands of years. They were able to monitor the deteriorating situation here on earth and I regret to say that our beautiful planet was virtually reduced to a wasteland, where only small pockets of human beings survived."

"So, you all understand why our future humans have been returning here for many years and have finally come forth here today, to endeavor to reverse that trend of mindless self-destruction and to give us all another chance."

"We blew it with our confusion of our politics and our religion, with our greed and with our lack of tolerance and understanding of the beliefs of others and of the very basic needs of others too – the people from impoverished nations."

"So what hope do we have to alter this known course of events and to change our destiny before it is too late?"

"We need to make some decisions, at international level, at national level, at community level and at every local level that we are all going to do our best to understand each other and to be more tolerant and flexible in the way we treat each other. We need to dismantle our weapons of destruction and to bring about a more equitable distribution of the world's wealth."

"As President of the United States of America, I say it is time for Muslim and Christian people to acknowledge the common ground in their beliefs, that the Prophet Mohammed be acknowledged by Christians as the prophet that he was, just as he, the Prophet Mohammed, acknowledged Jesus Christ as a prophet. Only now we know that Jesus did, in fact, rise from the dead as portrayed in the gospel. Needless to say, our community of Jewish people too, will need to accept that Jesus was who he claimed to be – the Son of God, their Messiah."

"Perhaps it is true that the words of Jesus Christ are the purest words ever spoken - his great commandment to love your neighbor as yourself and his sermon on the mount provide us with the formula for perfect social cooperation. But when you look at what people have taken those words and done with them over the eons – the Crusades, holy wars, mass murder, genocide, using religion for legalistic theft, etcetera – that is an indictment on human nature, it is not an indictment on the purveyors of good will – of Jesus Christ, the Prophet Mohammed, the Buddha and Confucius. We now have a second chance to live up to that great commandment of Jesus Christ – the golden rule - and to save our humanity here on earth."

"And so I say to you, people of the world, no matter where you are or no matter who you are, there is no longer any reason for us to torment each other the way that we have for so long. Muslim people should be free to continue praising Allah in the same way they have for almost fifteen hundred years and Christians should be free to worship God the Father, the Son and the Holy Spirit, for these are all one and the same – we all worship the same God."

"This will require the world's Islamic leaders to unanimously and unequivocally denounce all forms of violence against non-Islamic people and to emphatically advocate love for all people, the same way that all Christian religions do."

"It is now clear that God did create us human beings as unique in his universe. Life here on earth started to evolve about ten billion years after the big bang and may have evolved elsewhere in the universe too, long before that. But God did create us in such a way that we could evolve into the only intelligent beings in this, our universe. God did give us our universe to explore, to colonize and to inhabit, but the universe is so vast that we will virtually take an eternity to make even a small impression on it. The Zircon people have estimated that there are several billions of habitable planets, that we humans have a God given right to explore and to colonize and to inhabit."

"You know, one of the last things that Zultan said to us before they left here today – he told us how they have managed to survive for so long. So I will tell you what he said. He said the entire fabric of their social structure is based on something they have found to be very powerful in nurturing social cooperation – and that is, forgiveness. Zultan has explained to me that on the planet Zircon their children are raised from a very young age understanding and practicing forgiveness. They have come to learn over many thousands of years that without forgiveness, acrimony and enmity will be rife within any community – usually for reasons pertaining to power and wealth."

"We all know how to forgive, but for some reason so many of us find it very difficult to bring ourselves around to doing just that. As you know this morning when we were gathered in the media room and waiting and hoping that this event would not turn hostile, waiting for an initial response from our friends, we in the media room said the Lord's Prayer. No! We did not just say The Lord's Prayer – we prayed to Our Lord, with the prayer that he gave to us. And it just occurred to me that there is just one line in The Lord's Prayer that actually requires something of us - and that is to forgive those who do us wrong. 'As we forgive those who trespass against us'. You know what that means don't you now? It means that for us to be forgiven by God for our own wrongdoing, we need to be prepared to forgive other people too. We need to forgive those who have done wrong to us, those who have hurt us. Perhaps the forgiveness of God toward us is contingent upon us being prepared to forgive others."

At this Michael turned to look at his wife Julie and she looked up at him. They both smiled and with a rather slow blink of the eyes and a subtle nod of the head, the expressed their concurrence with the President's remark. Michael then leaned forward and gave his wife a kiss on her forehead.

"But now I'm starting to sound like some born again preacher!"

Everybody laughed!

"So we need to invest far more resources into values education in our school system, we need to work on our values education and nurture our own children into being tolerant and into understanding others and into forgiving people. Perhaps our entire future depends upon this."

"Our Zircon friends have also divulged here today that they do conduct a lot of research into after life experiences or near-death experiences and they have told us that they have virtually irrefutable proof that a person's spirit does, in fact, live on after our human body dies. Some people have been brought back to life after many days of being apparently deceased and have accounted for their experiences over several days. They told of their experience in being able to traverse the entire universe to be anywhere at any time – even observing dinosaurs from the past of looking into the distant future. But they all felt immense happiness, peace and love."

"I must admit to being quite a fan of Dr. Eben Alexander and his book 'Proof of Heaven' which I read some time ago and I did have the great fortune of meeting Dr Alexander when he attended the awards for the American Literary Society. I must say I was very impressed with his vivid accounts of life after he apparently passed away and like so many others, I regard his accounts as being totally credible. So I do not find it at all surprising that a civilization that is far advanced on our own would devote so much scientific research into after life or after death experiences. After all, so much of what we, ourselves, have done in our short history has been in the pursuit of truth. In fact I think it is totally amazing that the Zircon people have developed that type of medical science to the point that they have and I certainly hope they can continue to research the afterlife. I am very keen to find out more about their results on this. Just imagine being able to traverse the entire universe in an instant and to see whatever you wanted to see in any galaxy or on any planet at any time in the past or the future. That would blow me away."

"As we know there are new galaxies and new stars forming on an ongoing basis and just as many dying out, but in our future we will have the technology that will allow us to abandon planets before they become uninhabitable. We will move on to new planets that offer us billions of years of peaceful and happy habitation."

"Now I need to return to something that I did allude to earlier. The Zircon people themselves did not develop the technology to travel backwards through time that has enabled them to witness this for themselves, but they received that technology from another human civilization far more advanced than they are - a civilization that visited them from the Triangulum Galaxy, which is approximately three million light years from Earth - and from a point of time about seventy thousand years into the future."

"They too, are us from our future - but are even far more advanced than our visitors here today are, by tens of thousands of years. They developed the technology that enabled themselves and the Zircons to travel backwards through time. Those people live on a planet that is about the size of Neptune, hence they have evolved – we have evolved on that planet - to be more than one hundred feet tall."

"Many of you would be familiar with the story of Gulliver's Travels. So I suppose they might have sent these little Zircon people here because they did not want to frighten us."

Everybody laughed!

"All of this starts right here, on our planet Earth and with us – but only if we can learn to live together in peace and harmony. We have a chance to ensure that we do not need to rely on the outpost on Mars for the survival of humanity. That is the way we are heading, but we can change all of that, with greater cooperation and the love for each other and the forgiveness of each other, that Jesus commands of us."

"The universe is our God given playground. Our universe will take us an eternity to explore!"

"Our universe - is our Garden of Eden."

Other publications by Michael Roses

"World of Words 500"

Essential words for professional level communication

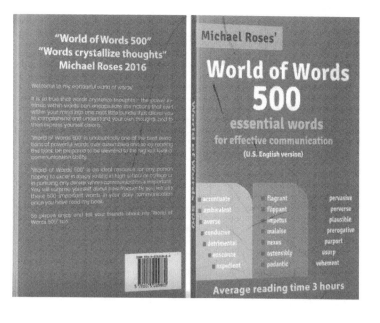